I0761847

ENTWINED

A Blackwood Tale

H. Sulfwin

TERRASECT

Published by Terrasect

Terrasect
PO BOX 3723
Norwich/NR7 7FA
www.terrasect.net

Publisher's Note: This is a work of fiction. Names, characters, places, and incidents are a product of the author's imagination. Locales and public names are sometimes used for atmospheric purposes. Any resemblance to actual people, living or dead, or to businesses, companies, events, institutions, or locales is completely coincidental.

Book Layout © 2017 BookDesignTemplates.com
Cover design and illustration by Jeff Brown Graphics
Map Illustration by FictiveDesigns

Entwined by H. Sulfwin. -- **1st ed.**
ISBN 978-1-83924-004-1
Paperback ISBN: 978-1-83924-105-5
eBook ISBN: 978-1-83924-106-2

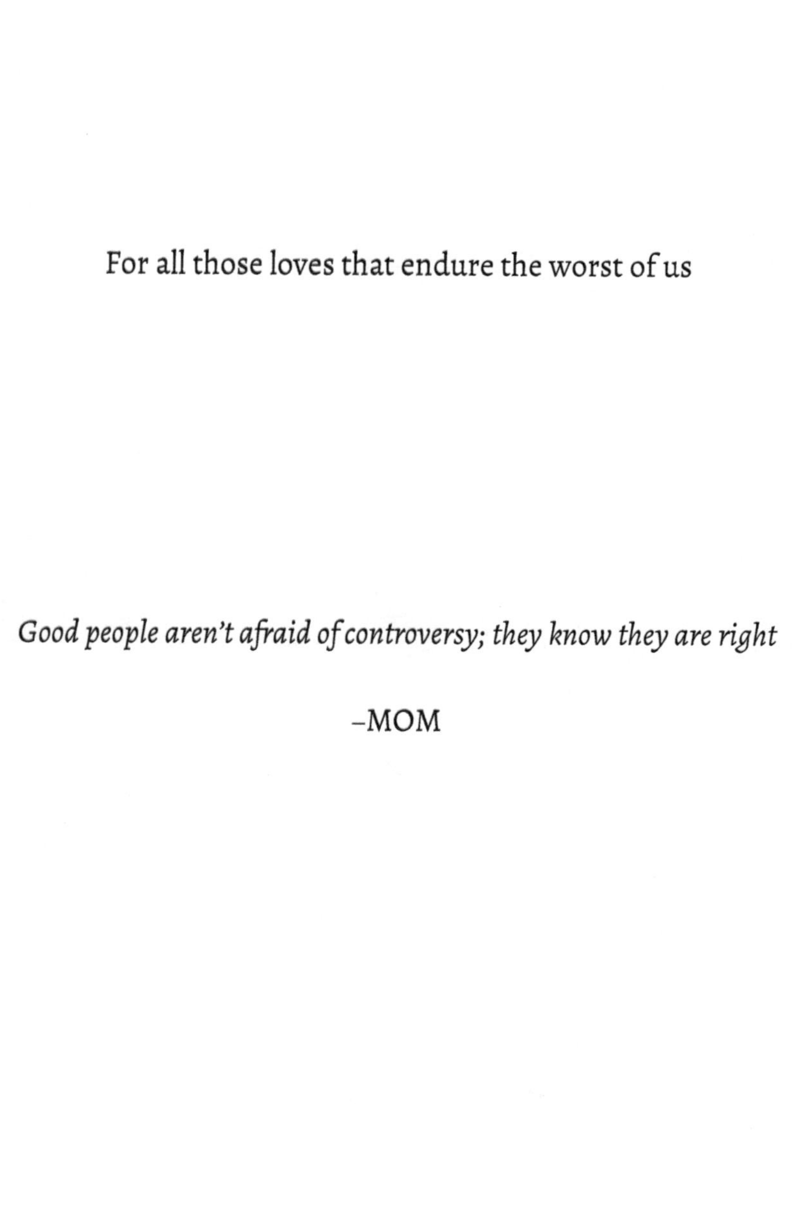

For all those loves that endure the worst of us

Good people aren't afraid of controversy; they know they are right

–MOM

CHAPTER ONE

ℋ

1452, 2ND Era Hamurfel, Akiro Region

The Dred King sat restlessly upon his ancient throne, growing more and more impatient as time went by; what had started as what he thought would be a minor and petty disagreement with the Orc Isles had grown into a fully-fledged feud, one that had so far been kept to words. To make matters worse, a sandstorm had blown in from the Akiron sandlands, smothering the midsummer harvest, and snapping the stems of young and sapling fig trees like brittle parchment with the continuous pelting of its fine, gritty particles. He beckoned over one of his servants and barked an order at the man to fetch him some wine; today was a day drink was needed.

Just as the servant scuttled away, a weary and storm-beaten messenger, her headscarf torn through though still covering her face, came rushing into the throne room from the blizzard of sand outside, hurriedly marching up to the King before kneeling before him.

"My King" she began, her voice rough and sore "the Lords of the Orc Isles have declined your terms. We are at war."

The King exclaimed, hammering his fist against the throne's armrest, causing the messenger to flinch.

Rising from the throne with purpose, he barked orders at the subordinates around him.

"-and you messenger, inform my agents; and have my Generals meet me here within the hour" his voice was harsh and angered.

"Yes my King" she bowed, before once again braving the storm.

The King marched through the castle's keep, the wine-fetching servant shuffling behind him, bottle in hand.

"How could they be so stupid" he thought to himself, enraged by the now enemy nation's leaders "over such pitiful land...Disgusting" he seethed out loud as he pushed open the stone door to the private chambers.

"What was that?" a soft and delicate female voice queried.

"Nothing important" the King replied, his voice markedly gentler than it was moments ago, cautious not to upset her.

He knelt beside the bed upon which she lay, her gentle shape just visible beneath the thin silk sheets covering her.

"Amira" he began, taking care with the way he spoke "the Lords of the Orc Isles have..."-he struggled for words momentarily-"...they have a situation, a...campaign of sorts, so you shouldn't expect a visit from Val'Ur for a while."

"Oh...You'll send her my love, won't you?" she gave a weak, if disappointed, smile.

"Of course, dear sister" he gave the false promise with a forced smile, physically pained by telling such a lie to her.

"I thought it had been a while since I'd seen her" a dry tear rolled down her cheek.

"Hey now" he spoke softly, gently wiping the tear from her face "Do not worry about her; she is strong and resilient. And you know how much she loves you"-he gave another forced grin-"You know how it is over there with their traditions; either join the campaign or bring shame upon your people."

She silently agreed, lightly clasping his hand, gazing into her brother's eyes as she did.

"Who...who is this campaign against?" she queried.

The King hesitated a moment.

"I...Yes, it was some marauder clan that had grown large enough to plague their shipping lanes. Rumour has it they're some separatist movement."

She seemed to accept that, though that was more likely due to her ill health than his ability to lie to her.

*

As he sat upon the Dred Throne, listening to his Generals and their plans for battle and espionage, he could feel the rage building inside, a seething disgust – hatred – towards the current state of things. He looked at the battle plans on the makeshift table before him, small statues representing the troops of his domain and his enemy cobbled together, acting out battles that have yet to happen. It made him think of all the death that would come from it, and the potential heartbreak of his sister.

"-if we were to eliminate – or capture – a number of the Orcish Lords, it could end the war before it has chance to escalate further" said General Xürr, a brilliant if young tactician whom had proved himself a worthy warrior in battle.

"Fool!" barked Zara, the oldest and arguably wisest of the Generals, who had served the King's father when he was upon the throne "Such tactics would prove to strengthen their resolve, give them a reason not to back down and to rally behind. Even the doubters in their ranks would fight for the life of their Lords."

"You are quick to call me fool, but it wasn't I who lost an entire battalion to a storm." Xürr mocked.

Such petty squabbles were not unusual in Hamurfel's upper class, even – especially – amongst its Generals.

Zara grew red with rage, but the King interrupted before she could speak.

"What if we captured Val'Ur?" he asked with his signature harshness.

The Generals looked at him, slight concern at such an idea coming over them – even if they could guess the why of it.

"My King, you suggest we take the Chancellor's daughter?" the question was asked by Aka Nor'un, a brutal warrior well known for even more brutal actions as a General; concern was unusual for him, but he felt that such a suggestion was tantamount to madness.

"Yes" the King looked at each of his Generals, picking up a statue representing enemy leadership off the map "I shouldn't have to tell you how much family can mean to a man"-he toyed with the statue a little as he spoke-"and the Chancellor is just a man."

"But sir, would that not make the Lords even more willing to keep fighting? As Zara said?" Xürr asked "Taking the Lords themselves is one thing, but a member of their royalty?"

"You question my judgment?" the King's voice grew harsher, but still controlled.

Xürr fumbled for words, struggling to think of a respectful response.

"I believe what General Xürr is saying" Zara interrupted, saving Xürr from himself "is that whilst we can debate as to whether the capture or executing of an Orcish Lord would help or harm the war effort, there is no doubt, no question, that such endeavours as kidnapping their royalty would result in...heavier conflict."-she gave a slight pause-"Especially one so beloved by their people."

The King stroked his chin thoughtfully, weighing up strategy against personal agenda.

"Prepare for me finalised battle plans, and send a second detachment to the settlements in Anirük." He rose from his seat, the Generals bowing courteously as he did "And make sure they include the capture of Val'Ur as a top priority" as he went to walk away he stopped and looked back at them "the safe capture of Val'Ur; make sure she comes to as little harm as possible, else it will not go down well with my sister, or me."

"Yes my King" the Generals saluted in unison as he walked off.

After the King had left the room, the three Generals looked at each other and the rough plans before them.

"Well" Xürr began "that's gone made this a hell of a lot harder."

"And dangerous" Zara said, eyes narrowed as she looked over the map "and potentially disastrous for us all."

Aka Nor'un shrugged uncaringly at this.

"At least if all goes wrong...well, let's just say the change in leadership could be worse."

They stared back at him with cautious anger.

"Watch your words Nor'un" Zara warned, barely holding back from seething "Such things could cause a man to lose his head."

He laughed at that, chuckling as he walked away.

"If anyone's going to lose their head, it'll be those that get in my way." He mocked as he left the throne room.

Zara and Xürr looked at each other.

"That was a threat, huh?" Xürr asked absently, his thoughts elsewhere.

Zara gave a silent nod.

"Better keep an eye on him" Xürr looked back at the statues upon the map "else we might lose this war from this side of the battle lines."

CHAPTER TWO

Ebo, Capital City of the Orc Isles Five months into the war

Val'Ur paced up and down the empty Council chamber. She was waiting for her father, Korren'Ur, Chancellor of the Lords of the Orc Isles, whom had been giving rallying speeches to the populous, maintaining and gaining more support for the war effort. She had protested against the conflict, seeing the action as nothing more than needless bloodshed; not that it affected her father's decision in the slightest. She had even appealed to the other Lords, but they were too concerned with gaining political favour with her father to listen, or too eager to exploit battle to line their own pockets with blood money.

She let out a sad sigh as she looked out of the stained-glass windows at the city below and its denizens scurrying about their business. It was alright for them, she thought, they didn't have their loved ones on the other side of the battle lines, nor did they have to carry the weight of all the dead and injured, or the horrors of the inevitable death and maiming that was still yet to come. She stopped pacing as she heard the great metal chamber doors open, and turned to face them as her father entered the room, two guards waiting outside as they closed the doors behind him.

"Greetings father" she called, her tone polite, if dry.

He gave her a brief smile.

"I'll get straight to the point Val" his tone was business-like as ever "Our strategists suggest this war could last quite a few years longer, and so-"

"Years?" she did not normally interrupt him, but this news came as quite the shock.

"Must I remind you of your manners?" he scolded.

"No, sorry father."

"You see those people out there?" he gestured to the window and the city below "Do you think they understand what war even is?"

She gave a glance at the people, noticing one pulling a particularly heavy looking cart, before returning her gaze to him.

"You see, we have only so many warriors" he continued "and most of the city folk are...let's say *unsuited* to a warriors life"-Val could sense her father was planning something unseemly for her, something she would profoundly dislike-"As such, it has been put forward by the Council of Lords that we lead by example, and encourage..."-he gestured absently as he searched for the right words-"...encourage matches of favourable breeding."

"With all due respect father, we cannot tell people who they can marry, or who to, to...who to mate with!" she was aghast, disgusted by the very idea.

"No, not make them; simply encourage. But to do so we must lead by example, as it were."

Val looked at him sternly, trying to find even the slightest bit of humanity in his expression.

"What are you suggesting here?" she asked, holding back her temper.

"Lord Tallon's son, he's about your age, and a good General-"

"You cannot be serious."

"Manners" he said dismissively.

"To hell with your manners! I will not marry someone I do not love, nor will I do so because you, or your strategists, say so!"

"You will be doing a great service for your people."

"By spreading my legs and shooting out a child?!"

"Val!"

"No father, I did not vote for this war, and I sure as hell won't betray my love for it!"

He scoffed at that.

"Love? You have no idea of what is important you impudent girl!"

"How dare–"

"No child, you will listen" he interrupted coldly "the way this campaign is going will drag it out for years – a great many years – and if nothing else we will need a steady supply of future warriors to replenish-"

"I will not-"

"-and we need the people to see their Lords and Chancellor united, and making the same sacrifices as them." he continued over her, exasperated "Look"-he moved to hold her, Val taking a step back as he did-"this is not about you, or me, not even the Lords, it's about them"-he pointed back out the window-"if they even sense that one of us is against the war you know full well that doubt would spread. Then where would we be? All that blood spilt, those lives lost, all of it would be for nothing."

She couldn't look at him, nor find words to say; she knew his tricks, his ways of manipulating people, she had seen him do it to others, but never her. Until now.

"I understand you're a little hesitant, and I understand it is hard to put aside your...crush on the Hamurfelion *princess*."

"A crush? A CRUSH?! She is my betrothed!" she snapped "She is the True Queen and my soulmate father, do you not understand? Hell, I'd wager you started this war just to keep us apart!"

He waved her off dismissively as he walked over to the metal doors, knocking on them to get the guards' attention, before then turning back to her as they opened.

"When you've finished this childish tantrum, think about your people, instead of yourself." With that he turned and exited the room, the guards closing the doors as he left.

Val stood there, a lone, solitary tear rolling down her toned skin, lightly smudging the face-paint upon her cheek, still staring at where her father had stood. The war had been hard for her before now, being so far away from her beloved Amira for so long, but with this added on?

She pulled out one of the cast-iron chairs from the stone table in the centre of the room, positioning it to look out of the window as she sat and thought.

She watched the people as they scurried along the roads and paths, down alleyways and across streets, as they carted goods, came and went, all the time thinking of her love in her otherwise distracted mind.

She dropped her head in her hand, knowing that despite her title and station, she had no choice – no free will – whilst she stayed here.

CHAPTER THREE

1453, 2ER
Cairngor, Disputed Lands
Six months into the war

The messenger darted from embankment to embankment, dodging volleys of arrows as she made her way across the battlefield. Her headscarf now hung down around her neck; this was no place to have her vision impaired, however slight. She took out her instructions as she knelt behind a wall of wooden spikes – a trap to stop the charge of heavy horse – before then peering out over its edge, looking from east to west, before finding her target; Commander Rahool, recognisable by his distinctive armour adorned with the leather of a great scaly beast.

She tucked the instructions back into a the small satchel they had come from, and once again readied herself to sprint between cover, counting the time between volleys of arrows whenever a target was spotted. When the next pause in the battle came she nimbly and elegantly sprung across the battlefield with the swiftness of a swallow, until at last she was in Rahool's fortified trench, barely avoiding a deluge of arrows, some embedding themselves in the wood she had just landed behind. Hearing noise behind him Rahool turned on the spot, his hand half-drawing his sword before realising it was her.

"Commander" she spoke calmly as she raised her hands, reassuring him she was indeed the King's messenger as he resheathed his sword.

"Messenger" his voice was gruff and sore from barking orders to his men "What news do you bring?"

"Not news"-she reached down into one of her pouches-"Orders" she said as she pulled out a folded piece of parchment, its battered and worn seal still holding it closed with the King's symbol.

The Commander took it from her, hastily breaking the seal and unfolding the parchment. As he read the orders she waited patiently, the sound of arrows and men shouting, the sound of metal hitting metal and of pain filling the silence.

"You are aware of what's in here?" Rahool asked as he looked up from the parchment.

"I am."

He gave a frustrated sigh as he rubbed the sweat from his brow, exhausted from commanding two units, and now exasperated by this additional set of orders he had to contend with. He handed the parchment back to her.

"Wait in the mess hall"-he gestured to a hobbled and hastily made wooden shack a good hundred yards back from where they were-"I'll send two swordsmen for you when night settles in."

She gave a silent bow before leaving him, making her way back across the battlefield.

*

The night had brought a tense calm to the battlefield, the only sign of two opposing forces the dim campfires and arrow-cloaked trenches left over from a day of war. She could just hear the sound of a drummer entertaining troops in the distance as she sat on the floor of the shack, leaning back against its northern wall as she dipped half stale bread into her lukewarm water. She took a bite of the soggy thing, excess water dripping down her chin. As she chewed she thought on the journey ahead, thinking on different scenarios, and how she would deal with them if they arose, as well as what routes she would take. The wait had been tortuously tedious for her, for she was used to being continuously on the move – only stopping on her terms and never for long – but for the King she could handle being restless for a few hours.

The sound of footsteps echoed in from the direction of Rahool's camp, and she stuffed the last of her soggy bread into her mouth, hastily chewing it as she downed the last dregs of her bowl of water; it was going to be a while before she would be able to eat in such safety again.

As one of the swordsmen pulled back the thick fabric that covered the doorway she wiped her mouth and chin with the cuff of her sleeve.

"Messenger?" he asked.

She gave a silent nod.

"Follow me" he said as the other swordsman held the fabric back for them.

The moon held low in the sky as they moved slowly and stealthily towards the enemy lines, taking great care not to be seen by the sentinels watching for any night-time attack. As they drew close they crept behind a heavy horse trap, one swordsman now looking for something concealed between the wooden pikes.

"This is as far as we go" whispered the other swordsman as he squinted over the battlement, looking for signs of enemy activity in the moonlight.

"Here" the other swordsman, having found what he had been searching for, thrust a bundle of clothes and chainmail into her arms "Commander Rahool wishes you luck...this armour cost us two men, two good men; make it count."

"Understood" she assured him calmly as she put her enemies armour over her clothes.

The swordsmen watched as she walked over to the enemy camp, wondering what orders – and what motive – the King had given for her to risk so much.

***

She had been trekking through enemy territory for a week now, having initially stolen one of the Orc's horses. She was, and had been, avoiding the main transport lanes, and thus increasing the time it took to get to her destination, but she felt the choice paid off; after all, it was better to get there slightly later than increase her risk of being caught.

She was heading to Ebo, the capital city of the Orc Isles, and was to deliver a message on behalf of the King to his sister's lover; though she also had kill orders for certain Lords if the chance presented itself.

It hadn't sat well with her how the King withheld information from his sister, Amira the True Queen, although she knew his motives were without malice; he did not want to risk getting her stressed in her current fragile health.

As her headscarf blew in the air that rushed past her as she rode onwards, the messenger – always two steps ahead – contemplated what action a truly loyal subject would take, her thoughts diverting from this only when, after hours of riding, she saw the lights of a gated village; her only way to get to her destination.

She slowed her gallop to a gentle trot, carefully planning what words she'd use when she was inevitably asked questions. As she drew within throwing distance she could see the two guards manning the entrance gates; they were ragged, almost scruffy, with dirt stained armour and weary eyed from what must have been several nights of duty.

"Halt!" one called out to her as she came into view; she came to a stop sideways onto them, both hands on the horse's reins "Who goes there?"

"Just a humble messenger" she hummed pleasantly.

"A messenger? And where might you be headed?" he enquired, the other guard standing close to the warning bell.

"The capital; I have messages for the warriors families" she gestured to a bag of sealed letters at her side as she told a half truth.

The guard lifted a lit torch from its sconce on the gate and walked over to her.

"I have to check you over messenger" he spoke dryly "War-time regulations and that."

"Sure thing." She gestured nonchalantly.

He ruffled through her papers and the horse's armour, stopping as he found a small short-sword.

"Care to explain?" he asked as he pulled it from its hold.

"A girl has to protect herself on these dark roads. And as I said, these messages are from the warriors on the front, which means being on the battlefields, so..."

He gave that a moment of thought.

"Fair enough"-he handed the sword back to her-"Can't let bandits get hold of a pretty thing like you, can we?" he smiled.

"You flatter me" she grinned convincingly "perhaps when I return from the capital we can do this again." He gave a laugh as he waved her through the gates.

As she trotted through the streets looking for an inn for the night, she pondered whether she would be able to avoid that particular guard when she made her return trip; a bit of light flirting to get past is one thing, but a second encounter – in the way she envisioned it if he remembered her – would undoubtedly be problematic.

She jumped down from her horse and walked it over to a water trough, tying it to a post, before then entering the village's only inn: The Hammered Feather.

As she entered she was greeted by the sight of a homely, warm room with pinewood furniture lined with well-worn fur, the odd patron sleeping at the bar and tables, still grasping their tankards tightly. Behind the bar a lone barkeep was wiping down the counter with a damp rag, her hair frizzy from a long night's work.

"Excuse me innkeeper" the messenger spoke softly as she approached her.

"Evening stranger" she replied, wearing a forced, but not insincere, tired smile "What can I do for you?"

"A room for the night, if you have one."

The innkeeper looked over the room keys she had left hanging below the bar.

"We do indeed" she pulled one off its hook "That's ten gold coins, twelve with breakfast."

The messenger rummaged through her small purse, counting out the ration of coin in her hand; this was quite the expensive stay, but there was no other sensible options.

"Best it be just the room, thanks" she held out the handful of coin.

"Right you are" the innkeeper replied as she took the coin, quickly counting them before handing over the room key "Yours is the forth door on the left of the hall up the stairs...and leave that key with Edward in the morning; he'll be behind here or out front."

"Of course." The messenger smiled, before heading off straight to her room.

After locking her door, she sat down on the bed, its coarse woollen blanket audibly scratching against her leather pouches. Unbuckling her belt, she pulled out her locket with her free hand from beneath her shirt, placing her belt and its pouches on the nightstand beside her, before then closing her eyes in a moment of quiet reflection, the locket lightly cradled in her hands.

She thought on how she missed her, and longed to hold her once again, but caught herself before she could release a tear. She tucked the locket back under her shirt and lay back on the bed, one knee raised as she fiddled with the lockets chain. Finally she closed her eyes, and dared to sleep without thinking of her mission.

CHAPTER FOUR

Hamurfel
Akiro Region

Xürr absently tapped his fingers against the table with the new battle plans upon them. He was due to ship out with his troops within the week, with the aim of capturing the western flank of Cairngor, and hopefully drive the Orcish forces back at least a couple of leagues. He was nervous, but not because of the fights and battles to come, but rather the thought of leaving Aka Nor'un with only Zara to keep an eye on him; he had become more brazen with his words, barely veiled threats against the monarchy, warnings to keep on his 'good side'; the King seemed to turn a blind eye to it. That or he was blinded by the war, Xürr thought.

"General Xürr?" a female voice knocked on his door.

He turned to see Zara leaning against the doorframe in her casual nightwear.

"Zara." He turned back to the plans in front of him.

"Nor'un is repositioning the home guard."

That grabbed his attention.

"How worried should I be?"

"We have time, of that I'm sure. But if your forces are away too long...I'm not sure my garrisons could hold back a revolt."

"Oh? Not like you to doubt your strength."

"We are too low on numbers, seeing as most of my troops are on the front lines."

He got up from his seat and walked over to her.

"We should talk to the King." He whispered "Let him know what Nor'un's been saying."

"You think that has not crossed my mind? He is blind to Nor'un's antics, and not just because of his sister; their having grown up together makes them like old friends to him. Makes me nervous it would be our heads on the line if we force a confrontation without outright proof."

Xürr gave a heavy sigh as he rubbed his eyes.

"If it wasn't for this damned war..."

"Xürr, that land is *ours*, ours to farm, ours to mine; it is our duty to protect it, for all of Hamurfel."

"It's not that. Nor'un...he's too dangerous in this climate."

She gave a silent nod, agreeing with that sentiment.

"How's the wife?" Xürr asked, changing the subject, feeling the need to take a break from his train of thought.

"She's alright...thanks for asking" Zara wasn't one for small talk.

"You found a suitable man to give you two a child yet?" he smirked.

She gave him a scornful look,

"Don't you dare offer again."

"Knew I could still pull your strings" he laughed.

She rolled her eyes at him.

"Just be ready to bring our forces home at a moment's notice, okay?"

"Of course" he was back to being serious, his face now a sombre one.

The two stood in silence a moment.

"You think he'd really do it?" He asked at last.

She gave a weary shrug.

"I don't think we can take that chance."

CHAPTER FIVE

Orcish Village
Southern Cairngor

Tara woke up as the new dawn sun shone through the small window on the far side of the room, and as she stretched she pushed the blanket off the end of the bed, the curls of her brown-red hair shifting over her shoulders and across her pillow as she turned her head to look toward the light. She lay there a few minutes, going over her plan of action for the next few days as the rest of her body woke up, one hand lightly resting upon her locket.

Putting her belt on as she got up, she checked its pockets, making sure they were still secure and their contents safe, before then picking up the room key and making her way down to the Inn's bar.

As she descended the steps, each giving off its own unique, dull creak, she was greeted with a smile from the man – whom she assumed was Edward – behind the bar, whom had looked up from his work as her heard her approach.

"Morning" he called out politely as he put down the cloth he had been using to polish the tankards with.

"Morning" she replied as she walked up to him, placing the room key on the counter "just returning this."

"Sure, sure" he nodded as he hooked the key back on its hook "Anything else we can do for you before you depart miss?"

"No...Actually, I don't suppose you would know which road is patrolled by the most soldiers?"-the barkeep raised a questioning eyebrow-"It's just, a lone lady such as myself must take the safer route; I've heard rumour of bandits around these parts." She was quite convincing as she spun false truths.

"Of course, of course" the man said, seeing the logic in that "I would say the north-eastern passage; it's a tad longer but definitely the safest route I'd say."

"Thank you" she smiled with a tilt of her head, before then walking out into the morning sun.

As the light hit her eyes she took in a deep breath of fresh country air; so much better than the dusty, sand-laden atmosphere of Hamurfel, she thought. As she strode towards her horse she could not help but think how easy it was going so far, although she was sure it would soon become much more difficult and dangerous when it came to sail over to the Orc Isles, and make her way to Ebo.

CHAPTER SIX

Ebo
Capital City of the Orc Isles

Chancellor Korren stared out of the window of the Council Chamber, overlooking the denizens of the city. He pondered a while on how many he would have to conscript before the war was done, although he felt he could direct them into signing up; patriotism, after all, is a very good tool for manipulation. He turned around as he heard the great metal doors open behind him.

"Lord Tallon" he greeted him with a handshake "I trust you are well?"

"Yes, I am good, thank you" the lord's voice was craggy and broken.

"Excellent; then shall we get straight to business?"

"Very well"-Lord Tallon took a seat at the carved stone table-"You say you have a proposition for me?"

"Yes...I believe we have much to gain from a...mutual agreement." The Chancellor replied as he took a seat opposite him.

"I'm listening" Lord Tallon pulled an apple from one of his pockets with his pudgy fingers as he spoke, taking an overly large bite out of it as he did.

Korren leaned forward, his fingers pressed together.

"Am I right in thinking your son – the General – is looking for a bride?"

"Indeed" Tallon spoke with a mouthful of apple, the sound of it mushing upon his teeth loud and agitating.

"Well, my daughter could be persuaded to be...receptive to any proposal she gets."

"Isn't she a woman-fancier?" Tallon scoffed, his rotund frame jostling against his clothes as he leant back.

"That is of no relevance or consequence; she will do what is right and good for her people."

Lord Tallon rubbed his bulbous chin thoughtfully as he chewed another mouthful of apple.

"What favour are you after Chancellor? I am not blind, nor stupid; this has nothing to do with encouraging the people to breed."

"Ah, I do like that cover story though" he chuckled, before returning to a serious tone, leaning in close with a whisper "I need this war to last, and I do not expect the people to keep supporting it based on some claimed land alone."

"Tread carefully Chancellor, I sense you may say something...unfortunate."

"I'm just saying, having a grandchild who would be the heir to the Chancellor's throne, it would be most beneficial, would it not?"

"It would."

"And would it not be a tragedy if a small town of civilians were to be massacred, slaughtered by our enemy in cold blood?" a cruel smirk etched itself upon his face.

Tallon stopped chewing, the slightest shock at the implied plan.

"Would we not need to retaliate in kind?" Korren gestured.

The pair stared at one another in silence a moment, each one weighing the other, Korren trying to work out whether or not he had made a misstep as Tallon slowly chewed the last of his apple.

"It would be...unfortunate." Tallon said at last, breaking the silence "though it would certainly galvanise the populous towards the war effort like nothing else."

"Indeed."

Tallon rose from his seat and made his way over to the chamber doors, before stopping and turning back to look at the Chancellor.

"Your motives are a mystery to me; just see to it your daughter has 'talks' with me before the marriage."

"Of course, Lord Tallon."

As the doors closed behind Tallon as he left, Korren looked back out the chamber's window, smiling to himself.

"Unfortunate for you my daughter" he whispered aloud to himself "but gloriously profitable for me."

***

The Royal Chambers, Chancellor's Palace

Val'Ur paced down the Palace halls, a silent and composed anger etched upon her face; she'd be damned if she was going to be used as some political pawn – if such an indignity, such abuse, could be called such. Beside her walked her handmaiden, a loyal – if quiet – servant called Roselia she liked to call her friend, whom was carrying blank scrolls, a quill and a sealed bottle of ink tied to her belt. As they came to the engraved door of Val'Ur's room she threw it open, almost taking it off its hinges, walking straight over to the small cabinet where she kept whiskey bottles she shouldn't have. As she drank straight from a previously opened bottle Roselia closed the door and locked it, before proceeding to lay out her materials upon a mirrored desk.

“I assume this is off the record Val?” Roselia asked, ditching the formalities as she unsealed the ink pot and dibbed her quill.

“Of course Rose”-she took another deep swig of the peaty liquid, perhaps too much as she pulled a face-“Do we have a messenger I can trust to deliver it?”

“Aye; Ji’Roh” Roselia replied as she unfurled the parchment before her, readying her hand to write.

Val paused her pacing.

“Your husband?” she questioned, worried “Rose my dear, perhaps I should explain more clearly what I’m asking.”

Rose turned to her with a gentle smile.

“I understand Val – truly I do – that is why he’s the only one – and I mean *the* only one – we can trust with this.”

“Rose...I...thank you” Val said as she gave a one armed hug to Rose from behind.

“Now how formal should this message be? Familiar yet fond?” Rose asked as she rubbed Val’s hand comfortingly with her free hand.

“Quite” Val replied as she planted a kiss on Roselia’s cheek, Rose giving her a concerned if comical look in return.

“That bad is it?”

“How could you tell?”

“You’re never that affectionate.”

Val pondered that a moment.

“Aye” she replied at last, before taking another swig of whiskey that was a bit too much.

CHAPTER SEVEN

North-Eastern Passage, Sojourn, Orcish lands

The wind whipped and whirled, lashing against her face as she galloped at full speed down the ill-kept road, a band of highwaymen attempting to chase her down. She had known it was going to be a risk taking the least guarded route, but it had been a calculated one – she had heard reports that the Orcish patrols were suspicious and paranoid over lone travellers, and she'd rather have her chance of capture as low as possible – but alas, the odds did not seem to be in her favour.

Her horse was near exhaustion, panting furiously as it weaved around a sharp turn and leapt over the trunk of a fallen tree. Tara looked back over her shoulder, seeing the highwaymen were still behind her and slowing closing the gap. She gritted her teeth, pushing her horse even harder, hoping to outspeed them long enough to run into an Orcish patrol; the irony of it was not lost on her.

She could hear them now, shouting between each other and at her, though she was too focused on escaping to hear their words. One of them broke ranks and managed to get close enough to make a grab for her with his dirty hands. She managed to doge his attempt, balling her right hand into a fist and swinging it back at him with all the force she could muster, catching him in the left eye and causing him to lose his grip on the reins of his horse and fall to the ground at high speed.

She felt fear trying to build up in her stomach.

'Too close' she thought 'far too close.'

Her horse began to lose speed; the poor creature was close to collapse.

'This is it'-panic was taking hold of her thoughts-'This is where it ends...why? Of all the things and places, why HERE?'-her brow furrowed-"No, not today."

She pulled back on the reins sharply, causing her horse to rear up and stop suddenly, almost throwing her from it, the highwaymen rushing past her, going too fast to stop in time.

As they slowed down to turn back to her she unsheathed her short-sword and gave her horse a kick, charging at them, her sword raised high at arm's length above her head. With fierce aggression she fell upon them before they had time to react, cutting through the shoulder of the one on the far right, removing him from the conflict in an instant. As she turned to face them once more they hastily drew their worn weapons and began to gallop at her, enraged that their prey was fighting back.

"You think you can take a woman?" she shouted ferociously "Well, COME ON THEN!"

She raise her sword high once more, and charged at the remaining four highwaymen, her face painted with adrenalin and nervous rage.

As she drew close to them they turned as fast as they could and ran. Confused and relieved, Tara returned to a gentle trot before finally coming to a stop, happy to give her horse the chance to catch its breath. As she let out a heavy sigh of relief she heard someone let out a loud laugh.

"My, you sure have some guts, girl!" an older female voice called.

Tara looked behind her; a patrol of four Orc warriors trotting towards her.

'Now I run into Orcs. Typical.' She thought to herself "Could have done with you four a couple of minutes ago" she called back to them with a smile, if a bit breathless.

"You seemed to have it under control" one of the male Orcs laughed as they drew up beside her.

"So you alright then?" the older woman asked.

"Yes, thank you; a bit shaken, but...just glad you showed up."

"It's why we're here. Speaking of, what makes a lone lass such as yourself take this road? Didn't you know how few patrols come this way?" she questioned, the tinniest hint of suspicion in her eyes.

"I had heard it was the shorter route, and I have these messages to deliver to the capital" Tara gestured to her bag as she lied "From the warriors on the front."

"Ah" she nodded "I understand your eagerness messenger, but next time take the safer path, even if it's longer."

"Oh I will, trust me."

"Quite" she smiled "Tell you what, Sierra here will travel with you up 'till the ferry port over to the Isles."

That caught Tara off-guard.

"Thank you, but I would hate to be such a burden-"

"No, no; we can't have the families back in Ebo not receive their letters and be left worrying now, can we? It would be negligent on my part to let you go off without a guard."

"I...I don't know what to say."

The older woman gave a hearty laugh.

"Keep her and those letters safe Sierra; you two, with me." with that she led the other two warriors off towards the village Tara had come from. She turned to Sierra.

"You sure this isn't inconveniencing you?"

"Not at all" she smiled "It'll be nice doing something a little more peaceful for a while, and I've got someone new to talk to."

"I guess it can get quite repetitive with just the four of you."

"You have no idea" Sierra laughed.

***

Five days later, Layla Hills, Sojourn, Orcish lands

The two of them sat around the campfire, Tara leaning back against a tree and her bedroll as Sierra toasted some crusty bread.

"So, you been to the front much?" Sierra asked as she turned the bread to toast the other side.

"A bit."

Sierra looked back at her.

"I guess it's not really the thing to talk about, all that death and blood."

Tara took her eyes off the stars above.

"I take it you've never been?"

Sierra shook her head.

"No. At first I was distraught at the idea of having patrol duties instead of fighting side-by-side with my brothers and sisters in arms, but lately...the stories I've heard, well, they're gruesome and grim."-She looked back at the fire-"Oh Damn!" she yelled as she pulled her now blackened toast from the fire's edge.

Tara giggled instinctively – much to her own shock – at the sight of Sierra desperately trying to scratch away the burnt bits without burning her fingers.

"What's so funny?" Sierra asked, mock serious as she took a bite of her half-salvaged toast.

"Oh, you just...you remind me of someone" she sighed.

"Oh?" she asked as she took another bite, crumbs sticking to the sides of her mouth.

Tara looked at her silently for a moment, a tad awkward.

"Oh...like that" Sierra realised as she wiped away the crumbs.

"No not...not-" Tara stammered.

"It's okay" Sierra said as she had the last corner of her toast "not like it 'ain't natural is it?"-she took a swig of her waterskin- "I...know someone that way inclined." She looked back at Tara, who was looking most awkward, and gave a wry smile.

"Close your eyes."

"What? Why?" Tara quizzed, still a tad paranoid that Sierra might have worked out her mission.

"Trust me, you'll like it."

"Like what?"

"That would spoil the surprise."

"Fine." Tara sighed as she closed her eyes.

A minute or so passed, the sound rustling fabric filling the quiet air.

"What are you doing?"

"You'll see." Sierra hummed.

"...Can I open my eyes yet?"

"Just a moment longer...okay, now open them." She purred.

Tara opened her eyes.

"Oh...wow...you're...wow."

***

Palace of the Dred King, Hamurfel, Akiro Region

The Dred King exited his sister's room, the servants tending to her gently closing the door behind him as he made his way down the corridor towards General Nor'un, who was patiently waiting for him.

"How's your sister my King?" he asked courteously.

"Stable...but in better spirits than usual."

"That is good to hear."

"I only hope this war is over before she gets better...or worse..."

"Keep positive my King, and all will be well" Nor'un smiled "It is the will of the Divines, I'm sure."

"You are good counsel my friend" the King patted him on the shoulder "Now, you say you have new thoughts on our tactics in Caringor?"

"Yes, may I show you?"

"Of course."

The two walked over to the newly appointed War Room, a centralised desk covered with a detailed map of the disputed lands, small statues which represented the positions of troops and units of battle upon it.

"As you can see, most of General Xürr's troops are holding the western edge of the front – having relieved Commander Rahool's second battalion, with General Xürr's Primary and Secondary Battalions now holding the northeast."

"Yes, reports from Rahool tell me they hold the line well."

"Indeed. However, I believe if we send the rest of General Zara's forces to spearhead a central assault we may – should – be able to capture anther or half-league or so."

The King furrowed his brow as he looked over his troops' positions.

"How so Nor'un? What makes now the time to launch such an offensive?"

"My King, look at the numbers we have"-he began moving pieces to show his idea-"If we can give them cause to charge forward in a bulk response, and have Xürr's eastern troops swoop around back of them and cut off their supply line to the front lines, we can then pierce it with Zara's remaining troops – perhaps with the heavy horse – then use her First and Second divisions to take the western ridge."

"And Rahool's battalions?"

"Supporting the central assault."

The Dred King rubbed his chin uneasily, knowing the stakes of such a risky manoeuvre, and how it would leave Akiro largely undefended.

"Do you have enough men to defend Akiro and the Palace if the worst were to befall us Nor'un?"

"Trust me my King, I have enough men to hold the Capital." Nor'un smiled

***

Layla Hills, Sojourn, Orcish lands

Tara awoke to the sounds of songbirds giving their morning calls, Sierra's arms wrapped around her, her head resting upon her chest. Slowly and gently as to not wake her, she pulled herself free from the embrace – resting Sierra's head on the pillow of her bedroll – and began to unwrap her clothes from her jacket, a soft wind cooling and caressing her naked form. As she got dressed Sierra stirred, stretching her arms as she awoke.

"Mornin' lover" she called gently.

"Er...morning" Tara replied, feeling most awkward and self-conscious.

Sierra looked at her a moment, detecting Tara's feelings.

"You alright?"

"Yes...here are your clothes" Tara threw the clothes to her in a fluster, an awkward silence falling between the two as they finished getting dressed and began to prepare the horses for the day's ride.

"Look, messenger-"

"Tara" she replied before she could stop herself, her thoughts quickly scolding her for telling Sierra her real name.

"Tara" Sierra continued "was...was I okay for you? I...I didn't do anything wrong did I?"

Tara looked at her directly for the first time since they woke, her ironclad barriers melting at the sight of genuine worry – or was it something more? – in Sierra's eyes.

"No...no you were great...perfect even" she sighed slightly.

"Then...we're okay? I haven't made this journey awkward for you?"

"No" Tara shook her head.

"...Tell me Tara, I can see you're troubled."

Tara leaned back her head against her horse's side. 'Come on Tara' she thought to herself 'she's a stranger – an Orc – and you have a mission'.

"Tara?"

A small tear rolled down her cheek as her eyes began to well up and her lips quivered.

"Tara?! What's wrong?" she put her arms around her instinctively, her natural empathy and compassion drawing her close.

"It's...I...I haven't..." she let out a choked sob, held back by a misplaced sense of shame.

"You don't have to tell me, just know that I'll listen if you need or want me to."

The two stood there as Tara cried upon her shoulder, until finally she took a deep breath and pushed herself off Sierra.

'Stupid' Tara thought 'How could I be so vulnerable, so...weak'.

Sierra looked at her, weighing her up.

"You're ashamed aren't you?"

"No...no that's not...it doesn't matter" she said as she adjusted her saddle.

"It clearly matters to you."

Tara bit her lip, trying to hold herself back from speaking.

"Fine." She relented, uncharacteristically unable to stop herself "You're the first...the first I've *been* with since my..."-'why are you telling her this Tara?' she thought as she spoke-"my dear Elisa." She felt her tears threatening to return.

"Your girlfriend?"

"My fiancé...oh sweet Elisa, how kind and gentle a soul she was..."

"You...lost her?" Sierra asked gently.

"Why am I telling you this?" Tara half laughed, and half cried.

"Well, I don't know about you, but for me"-Sierra moved in close-"it's because I felt a certain connection between us, and I guess you feel it too."

Tara looked back at her, thinking it over; perhaps this was her chance to finally let someone in, even if that someone was meant to be her enemy.

"I...she died in childbirth...as did our son"-she rubbed her face with her hand-"after all the risk and danger I put myself in, she dies in our home...it's cruel."

Sierra silently nodded, unsure of what to say.

"And after the indignity of finding a suiter to father the child! What backwards and cruel a world allows that? What uncaring forces must exist to inflict such misery upon her, upon me?" she threw her arms in the air angrily, though in part at herself.

"Well" Sierra began, turning Tara's face to hers "I cannot begin to imagine how much pain that has caused you, and continues to cause you, but – and I know we've only just met – I feel that this, *us*, we were fated to meet, to find one another."

"What are you saying?" Tara looked into her eyes, searching for something.

"I'm saying once you've – we've – delivered those letters of yours, perhaps we could...be something more?"

They looked at each other, each gazing deep into the eyes of the other. Tara gave a half disbelieving smile, momentarily lost in Sierra's mismatched blue and green gemstone eyes.

"I'd like that." She said at last.

Sierra smiled back, giving her a quick hug before jumping atop her horse.

"Well, come on then, haven't got all day you know" she chuckled.

As Tara mounted her horse she could not help but wonder what kind of trouble she had made for herself, and the difficulties that would ensue from it; but as she looked at Sierra she decided that she might just be worth the risk.

CHAPTER EIGHT

Ebo
Start of the seventh month of War

Roselia held Ji'Roh tightly, making their embrace last as long as possible.

"Ji, promise me you'll not take any risks" she asked sweetly.

"Any more than I am?" he laughed, his fierce grin shining through his stubby beard.

"You know what I mean you fool" she joked.

“Aye, I do” he sighed “Can’t quite believe it’s come to this though Rose, I really can’t.”

“I know, but Lady Ur needs us; we cannot turn our backs on her.”

“Wasn’t saying we should” he caressed the side of her face with his right hand “I’ll be back before you know it; you have my word on that.”

She smiled back at him.

“Let it never be said I ‘aint loyal” he said as he opened the door to leave, turning back to face her “Love you Roselia. Tell Lady Ur about-”

“I will Ji, I will. Love you too” she replied, holding back a flutter of tears drawn from her worry for his journey ahead.

With that he left, secret letters in the satchel on his waist, Roselia left looking at the now closed door.

She sat down on a chair beside the small fireplace, softly rubbing her belly.

“Well little one” she whispered “looks like it’ll be just the two of us for a while.

CHAPTER NINE

Cairngor, Disputed Lands

Xürr sat in his command tent, not five-hundred meters from the front lines, a lone candle lighting the dusk of midnight, the sounds of his patrols switching duties in the background. The fighting had grown worse, barbaric even; the longer the fight continued, and the more tedium set in, the worse it would continue to grow.

In his hand was a letter, brought to him by an exhausted scout, whom had said he was several days ahead of reinforcements and on the orders of General Zara. The letter was short and to the point, its last paragraph occupying his mind as he sat there:

Xürr, Nor'un has convinced the King to send all my troops – including myself – to the front for a full on assault, positioning his men throughout the Capital and placing them on guard duty for the whole royal family. I am no longer able to keep them safe. I fear we are about to be sacrificed – alongside our troops – in a purposeful loss; it is only then that Nor'un could make a play for the crown without much rebellion, as it would seem a reluctant but necessary action to safeguard our people from further loss.

Buy us time.

It was during this quiet contemplation that Commander Rahool entered his tent.

"Rahool" he greeted him as he turned in his chair to face him.

"General Xürr."

Xürr handed him the letter, and after a brief moment of reading, Rahool let out a series of angry profanities.

"That...that damned traitor! Damn him to Oblivion!"

"Quite" Xürr replied calmly, fidgeting with a stick of charcoal.

"What's our move?" Rahool asked his old student.

Xürr looked back from his thoughtful gaze.

"Depends; I figure we strike them from the east, using heavy horse to draw their archers' attention, then retreat as we send in horses loaded with tar and oil from the north-western side and set their ranks ablaze."

"Not bad, but it seems too cruel an action to take."

Xürr raised a questioning eyebrow.

"Not like you to feel compassion for our enemies" he said.

"I'm not; it's the horses I'm concerned about."

Xürr laughed; then an idea came to him.

"Goddamn! That's it! We build a catapult!"

"Xürr you twisted bastard, I love it!" Rahool grinned wildly "I'll get my men right on it"-he went to leave the tent-"Just leave my horses alone, okay?"

Xürr gave a slight shrug.

"If you insist. But we don't need perfection with the catapult, just good enough to disrupt whatever deal Nor'un has with the Orcish Lords."

Rahool nodded, before ducking out of the tent, leaving Xürr alone once again, tapping his stick of charcoal against his table in thought.

CHAPTER TEN

The North-Eastern Pass Orcish Lands

Tara looked over her headscarf as Sierra tied their horses to a tree, thinking upon home. It had been a gift, a cherished one in a way that left it well used and worn; now wasn't the time to wear it however – orcs rarely wore headwear, especially something distinctly Hamurfelion – but still, it was nice to feel its fabric between her fingers.

"You alright?" Sierra asked, seeing her mind was clearly elsewhere.

"Hm?" oh, yes; just thinking on times past"-she tucked the headscarf neatly away-"You sure this is a good spot to stop for the night?" she asked, changing the subject.

"Aye; these trees should provide us ample shelter, and we're far enough from the road to avoid any trouble that comes through."-she began unpacking her bedroll-"So, Tara, from where in the Isles do you hail?"

Tara knew she was only being polite – or perhaps simply curious – and not probing her out of suspicion, but she would have to make a lie of the truth all the same.

"Hard to say really" she began, leaning back against a tree as she pulled a half-chunk of bread from a satchel pocket-"we were always on the move when I was growing up; mother never did say where 'home' really was."

"Military or merchants?"

"Neither" Tara smiled at the corner of her mouth; the best lies were always true in part "If you really want to know, my family moved around to find work and to get away from trouble"-Sierra raised an eyebrow at that-"Ma would always say it was because she got restless – had to 'see it all, experience everything' she would say – and da, heh, he would almost ensure we couldn't stay in one place for long; he wasn't a bad worker or anything, but trouble always found him...or the other way around"-she chewed a small piece of her bread-"Honestly, I'm surprised he never ended up in irons the way he carried on."

Sierra thought on that a moment – now sat cross-legged upon her bedroll as she listened attentively to Tara's words – her eyes catching Tara's focus as she turned to look at her; their green and blue seemed almost mythic in nature.

"Forgive me, but are saying your father was some kind of miscreant, like a thief or scoundrel?" she enquired, her tone amazingly empathic for a stranger.

"Tara gave a laugh, in part at how she could only speak of her past inside of a lie, in part at how little of what she said was untrue.

"Not a thief, no; just a man that used up all the goodwill folk would give him, all in his desperate attempts to make some coin fast. Hilarious thing is, had he put the same effort into an honest profession – being an honest person – he would have had much more. We would have had so much more."

She sighed at the end, biting the side of her mouth absently at wanting to change a thing that had already been.

"So how'd you end up a messenger going to-and-fro from the front lines?"

"Well"-Tara walked over and sat in front of her-"I'm loyal for one thing – to our people more so than our leaders"-she had almost said 'our King', her feelings for Sierra, whatever they were, were begging for her to be honest; but she had a mission to do, so lie she must-"I worked hard for the trust that has been bestowed upon me, took me years of running between cities carrying messages and secrets of all kinds, until I ended up here."

Sierra had leaned forward, if just a little, her hands resting in her lap as she listened intently to Tara's every word; she seemed captivated by her, fascinated, and if Tara was honest with herself, she was more than just a little happy to have those mismatched gemstone eyes focused solely on her.

"But how did you start?" Sierra asked, intrigued "How do you go from being dragged across the land by your family to being a trusted messenger for the military? There must be a beginning there."

"Sure" Tara nodded, tearing another small chunk off her bread piece before offering some to Sierra-"Fact is, as soon as I was able I walked – no, I'll be honest; I snuck into a General's office and made my case."

Sierra pulled an expression of incredulity, forgetting the bread piece in her hand.

"You snuck into a General's office? How didn't you end up in irons?"

"Well, I assume for most people that's the way it would have gone, and perhaps if it had been any other General I might have been, but it would seem I made a good impression; if I might say so, he seemed most impressed at my stealthy abilities."-she paused as she pulled off another piece of bread-"He did warn me not to do it again though, and by warn, I mean explain just what ill fate it would bring me."

"I bet he did" Sierra smiled "What luck though, really"-Tara just gave a shrug-"So, your parents, what became of them?"

Tara stopped chewing a moment, pulling her waterskin from her belt and taking a sip before answering.

"Gone."

Her tone was unmistakeably different from before; Sierra knew – whatever or however it had happened – that she would not share that tale.

"I'm sorry to hear that" Sierra shuffled forward slightly, placing a hand upon Tara's knee in an act of comfort.

Tara looked down at Sierra's hand cautiously.

Then, in an act of defiance to her usual distancing ways, placed her hand upon the back of Sierra's.

"Thank you" she smiled, genuine if sombre.

The two looked into each other's eyes, losing track of time for a moment or two.

As they snapped out of their shared moment, realising it had begun to get too dark to stay awake, Tara realise she had begun to feel something dangerous and hopeful: love.

CHAPTER ELEVEN

Chancellor's Palace Ebo

Val'Ur walked barefoot into her private bathing chamber, wrapped in a fluffed cotton gown. Scented candles lit the room brightly, the intricate and ornate carvings and engravings shining in their enamel colours.

She looked at the warm, frothed water, sighing in relief at its crystal blue colour and the warm haze that drifted from it and wafted the sweet scent of soaps dissolved within it. She let her gown fall off her with little effort, it dropping to the floor with a silent thud, allowing the warm air to caress her body as she lightly dipped a toe in to test the water; she smiled to herself, the temperature was just perfect. With that she lowered herself in, feeling the water envelop her in its warm embraces, a feeling of deep release and pleasure flowing through her. Using a soft sponge to wipe away her face-paint, she relaxed into the sense of freedom and bliss that came from these rare naked moments; and not just in the literal sense either.

It was the vulnerability of it, and how – within these walls at least – she felt truly safe, as if this was what life was meant to be, meant to feel like. As the last of her paint came off and she rinsed her sponge, she regarded her naked frame in her refreshed eyes as she let her hair down. She had an athletic build – something not unusual for a member of the Chancellor's family – one that radiated physical strength and finesse, but she did wonder whether Amira would still see her as the same girl she had fallen in love with those years ago; whilst she had always been athletic and muscular in build, she had become much more so since the last time they had been together. She closed her eyes a moment, listening in on the sounds of her own heartbeat, focusing on it and the sensation of the warm ripples flowing over and against her as she slowly waved her hands through its almost silk-like texture. There was no façade here, no mask of public appearance – nor political theatre – not even the pretence of the so-called 'high class' formalities and traditions, just her and the clear waters that enveloped her, and the hand carved soaps and sponges that cleansed her of the day's filth – both actual and figurative.

She smiled as she thought of her fiancé, her sweet Amira; how she missed her, that sweet smile and dainty frame of hers, how she missed holding her hand as they walked the Citadel's halls, or being wrapped in each other's arms on a cold winter's night. She winced as she thought on how her father was engineering things to force her into marrying Lord Tallon's son for his own ends. She let out a heavy sigh as she opened her eyes to the sound of a light knocking at her door.

"Who is it?" she called in a half weary voice.

"Roselia m'lady" came the answer in a sweet and uplifting tone "May I enter?"

"You may."

Rose unlocked the door with her spare key, entering the room with her back against the door as she carried a basket full of fresh clothes and towels, gently placing it down to relock the door.

"How is your bath Val?" she asked as she placed out embroidered towels and silky nightwear on a seat and shelf across from Val.

"Most enjoyable" she smiled as she stretched her arms behind her head "Oh, if only I could live in these waters."

Rose gave a small chuckle.

"You are most funny m'lady."

Val looked over at her.

"...Any news?" she asked, the tiniest hint of concern in her voice.

Rose stopped what she was doing for a moment.

"No, I'm afraid not Val."

Val returned her gaze to the ceiling.

"I guess it all takes time" she muttered, letting her mind drift a little.

Rose came over and knelt beside the bath.

"Val, I have some other news, about my...situation."

Val sat up.

"Oh?"

"Well" she began, absently taking Val's sponge and washing her back for her "it would seem that I'm with child."

Val's eyes and smile widened.

"Rose, that's most wonderful!" she leaned over and gave her a wet hug "Congratulations!"-she relinquished her from her grasp-"Oh Rose, had I known I would never have asked-"

Rose grasped her hand softly.

"Val, it's okay; I know if the roles were reversed you would do the same in a heartbeat. I mean, you're my best friend – my sister-in-arms – what else would I do?" she smiled.

"My position, that I am the Chancellor's daughter, didn't pressure you at all did it?"

She shook her head.

"My loyalty is to *you*, not your rank."

Rose continues to sponge down Val's back as they sat there in silence a moment.

"So...you hoping for a boy or a girl?"

"So long as they're healthy, I don't care which they end up being."

"But if you had to choose?"

Rose rolled her eyes.

“What of you and Amira?” she asked in an attempt to shift the conversation “Are...were you two thinking of children before...?”

“I’m not sure” Val bit her lip thoughtfully “I mean, after this war is over perhaps...but I’m not all that bothered about having children. Amira on the other hand loves them dearly; I remember when I was on a diplomatic visit to Hamurfel where she showed me an orphanage in their capital, Akiro, and how she looked at them as she doted upon the poor things as if they were her own.”

“So she would want one of her own?”

“I...we haven’t really talked about it, truth be told.”

Rose continued to wash Val, humming away as she did, Val contemplating some far-off plans yet to be set in motion.

“Rose, would you like to join me in here?” she asked suddenly and nonchalantly.

“M’lady?” Rose blushed in shock.

Two close friends bathing together and washing one another was not unusual in Orcish culture, where the bonds of friendship were strongest, but for two people of differing rank to do so? That was unheard of.

“It’s just, with your condition – as you put it – it would be unjust and improper to not let you be as pampered as I” she smiled.

Rose raised a questioning eyebrow.

“Is that so?”

“Indeed; and don’t let etiquette stop you.”

“It just seems...strange.”

“How so?”

"Because it's *you!*" Rose chuckled "You've never been so...so soft! Always the fierce, strong lady of stone."

"Perhaps, Rose, I can be strong and caring, hard and soft; people are nuanced creatures after all" Val scoffed light-heartedly "I dare say caring *is* strong, in its own way."

Rose fidgeted indecisively for a moment.

"The water is still nice and warm" Val hummed.

"Well, I guess it beats the old tin bath in front of the fire" Rose shrugged as she began to undress, Val sliding over to let her in.

As rose dipped her feet in and lowered herself she felt intense relief in her joints and ankles as the silky waters ran over her.

"Oh my! This water...it feels...different, nice, but different."

"It's those exotic soaps, they make the water feel thicker don't they?"

"And smoother" Rose replied as Val rubbed her back with the sponge.

After a while the pair were laid back, Val's arm wrapped caringly around Rose's side.

"...I'm glad I have a friend like you Rose" she said quietly, in a highly unusually soft voice.

"And I you" Rose replied as she leaned her head back on Val's shoulder "You miss her don't you?"

"Deeply" she muttered "I miss holding her."

"I understand"-she gently held Val's hand-"Ji'Roh has been gone only a short while and I already miss him dearly; to have your love separated by a battle line for this long...it must be agony, and my heart bleeds for you."

"...thank you Rose."

Rose turned on her side to face Val, looking deep into her eyes.

"Is this why you're not your usual stone-walled self?"

Val looked back at her silently, her eyes telling Rose her answer.

"Well, if you'd indulge me, m'lady" Rose began as she snuggled close to her friend "as it can get unsettling being by myself during the nights, could I perhaps lodge in your quarters with you, so I might feel safe?"

Val looked at her knowingly, seeing her friend's kindness as plain as day, and most thankful for it.

"Oh Rose...if I weren't already made of stone you'd be my rock" she smiled, holding back her emotions, though only a little.

They lay there a while as the water began to cool.

"So...I'm guessing we have only one set of towels?"

"Yep."

"Huh" Val looked at the ceiling tiles absently "well, that's going to be awkward."

"You mean it isn't already?"

"Fair point."

CHAPTER TWELVE

ℋ

Featherview Hills, North-Eastern Pass, Sojourn, Orcish Lands

Many nights had now passed since Tara and Sierra had joined each other on the journey to Orcain – and more specifically Ebo – with them both finding themselves growing ever fonder of the other, now passing the shores of a calm, shallow stream-come-river.

Tara was watching the water they had gathered from it boil as Sierra let the horses drink, the sun warm but not scorching, a waft of parted, veiled clouds curving to the east.

Sierra had removed her armour, which lay next to Tara along with her socks and boots, wearing only her under-armour with her leggings rolled up to just below her knees as she waded into the shallows.

"How's the water?" Tara called to her, silently appraising Sierra's strong but feminine frame.

"Cool" she replied, one hand holding the horses' reins as they drank heartily "You should join me."

"Then who would watch the water boil?" Tara joked; Sierra just gave a shrug, then returned her attention to looking at what may lie beneath the water's surface

Minutes later Tara was filling the last of their waterskins with the boiled water, carefully and slowly pouring as not to spill any, the horses now loosely tied to a group of saplings, as Sierra waded through the water, picking out shimmering pebbles and rocks that took her interest.

"We can't take them all, you know" Tara smirked, taking a sup of the remaining boiled water as Sierra waded out of the stream and came over; Sierra stuck her tongue out, mock serious.

"I know"-she turned to look back at the water, having placed a speckled rock of grey, quartz and pyrite at Tara's feet-"Don't suppose we have time for a bathe?"-Tara gave her a look-"I know we need to get to Ebo as soon as we can, but I wouldn't be long, and it'll be a while before we get anywhere we can bathe in private."

Tara rolled her eyes.

"How long you going to be?"

"Not long" Sierra chimed, taking off her top and throwing it at Tara "Just watch my things...unless you want to join me of course."

Tara stared after her as she held Sierra's clothes, unsure of whether this was flirting or Sierra's cheeky sense of humour.

Ultimately, Tara decided there was only one way to find out.

***

Falketh, Orcish-Bahvain Border

Ji'Roh had had no choice but to take a much longer route to the Court of Hamurfel, for he had to deliver another message to the son of the Orcish Lord Kaymar Ul'Sün, who also had the name Kaymar (Kaymar Ul'Sün the seventh, to be exact), whom he would find at the Orcish-Bahvain border. Kaymar was what Roselia had called 'one of the good Lords', and was a trusted friend of Val'Ur. His mission was a dangerous one, but both his honour and his love for his dear Roselia kept him determined and assured he was doing the right thing. He was in good spirits, and making good time when he arrived in Falketh, the large city like town that sat on the border between the Orcish and Bahvain lands in a valley of the northern Sojourn Mountains, and had promptly found the embassy of Kaymar.

"My Lord" Ji'Roh greeted Kaymar as he gave a bow and knelt before him "I have an urgent and private message to deliver to you."

"And who sent this message?" Kaymar asked, intrigued.

"Val'Ur."

“Oh”-Kaymar rose from his seat-“Walk with me, messenger of Val’Ur.”

With that Ji’Roh followed him to a secluded study, free of guards and diplomates.

“What troubles Val?” Kaymar asked as he gestured for Ji’Roh to take a seat.

Ji’Roh handed him a sealed letter, which he promptly opened and read, one hand rubbing his chin as he did so. Ji’Roh watched, silently waiting for him to finish, gauging his thoughts by the changing expressions upon his face.

“This is indeed troubling” Kaymar muttered as he finished “I trust you are aware of the situation?”

“Only the basics; as I am married to Val’Ur’s handmaid I have been trusted to deliver the message, but I have refrained from knowing much of her plan in case of discovery” Ji’Roh replied, a tad nervous as to whether Kaymar would aid them.

“Logical”-Kaymar looked back at the letter a moment, then back to Ji’Roh-“So you are to travel to the Court of Hamurfel next?”

“Aye.”

“This is a dangerous thing for an Orc. There is no guarantee they will not take you for a spy and act accordingly.”

“Aye, this I know.”

Kaymar let out a heavy sigh as he tucked the letter into an inside pocket on his jacket.

“I shall see about getting you a change of clothes, something of Blackwood origin, so that you might have a better chance of making your journey” he rose from his seat “I shall send word to Val'Ur that we are agreed; I will lend her my aid, but I shall need time to muster such a...resistance, as it were."

"Of course my Lord" Ji'Roh bowed as he got up from his seat.

"Heed my advice, do not travel the western road; take to the north, past Bahvil town and then west through Havai forest."

"What is wrong or dangerous about the wester road, if you don't mind my asking?"

Kaymar went silent a moment, before turning his voice to a barely audible whisper.

"There is rumour among the Lords, an order of sorts. I can help Val, or I can stop...we play a dangerous game, understand? Just know – and make sure Val knows – that I have not the choice, that I am powerless to stop this."

"Stop what?" Ji'Roh asked in a worried whisper.

"You'll hear about it, but it will be told in a lie. Val's words in that letter have cemented for me that our Chancellor is corrupt, and has equally corrupt Lords at his disposal; and I fear the rumours now to be true."

"My Lord, you're scaring me with these words."

"Good; now is the time to feel such things. But stay headstrong my good fellow, with Val's plans we are sure to bring our people out of this accursed war and into the light. Now travel safe, and if anyone asks, you brought me news on my mother's health, understood?"

Ji'Roh nodded in agreement, a mental itch making him want to take the western passage, just to see if what he thought was being implied was true.

'It couldn't be' he thought to himself as he was led to a changing area 'could it?'

***

Eastern Trade Route, Orcish Lands

They were now off the north-eastern pass, moving east through a tree laden landscape the orcs confusingly called 'The Clearing' due to its nestled location between two rows of mountains.

As their journey had progressed, they had grown to know each other a little better with each passing day, with Tara weaving fewer lies into her truths. It had made her think; these feelings she had, these feelings that – having been sparked by a moment of surprising but organic passion – grew and manifested in stronger and stronger sensations that at times felt like they might consume her, was it love she felt? Infatuation? Or simply a means – however desperate – to fill the void left, empty still, by her dearly departed Elisa?

But still she continued to allow Sierra to know her – how could she not when Sierra was so open and trusting? – and, if she were to tell the truth as to why, even if only to herself, she would have said it was because, no matter the cause, it felt *real*, right; the path she needed to tread.

As Sierra told a story from her early days as a warrior on patrol, Tara thought on how, other than Sierra's trusting voice and calming – soothing – way of speaking, it had been her eyes – one green as the brightest emerald, one blue as the purest, deepest sapphire – that had captivated her. It wasn't just in their unusuality either, but in the way they sparkled in their brightness and seemed to stare into her soul anytime Sierra looked her way; the way they widened with every smile, every laugh, Sierra gave was most enduring too. When Tara told Sierra what few tales she would, Sierra would sit quietly, listening with genuine enthusiasm, and those eyes of hers could hide nothing – they were too honest, if there were ever such a thing – and caused Tara to lose her will to hide behind lies. Sierra's expressions were easy to read, her mannerisms honest and clear.

It made Tara feel like a fraud.

She wanted something to come of this – of them – desperately so, but...she had given her word to her King, what else could she do but deceive this beautiful soul?

Tara snapped out of her thoughts as Sierra ordered her to wait.

"What-?" Tara asked, instinctively pulling back on her horse's reins as Sierra pointed to a ditched, upturned carriage.

The two watched it for a few moments.

"What do you think?" Tara asked "There's clearly no sign of its horses."

"Hmm" Sierra chewed the side of her cheek, thinking "I should check this out."

"But...?" Tara asked, sensing her hesitation.

"That's an expensive carriage."

Tara understood; no-one would leave something so valuable unattended.

"You thinking it could be an ambush?"

Sierra didn't answer; she was too focused on scanning the area.

"We'll have to pass it either way" Tara shrugged "What does your warrior's code tell you you should do?"

Sierra looked at her, a faint smile upon her face.

"I just want to make sure those letters of yours make it to Ebo in one piece; they're too important."

Tara could tell her concern was about more than just the letters.

"I don't mind leaving the carriage be if you don't" she said, giving the smallest of pauses before she continued "But...I don't want this troubling you later on."

Sierra felt the inflection in Tara's voice.

"Right" she nodded "We check it out, carefully."

They dismounted from their horses once they were almost next to the fallen carriage, Tara offering to climb atop it to look inside – reasoning she was more suited to do so, being unencumbered by armour as Sierra was.

Though she was more than capable of getting atop it by herself, she allowed Sierra to help her, her strong, gentle hands steadying her as she lifted herself up.

As she looked inside she heard movement, followed by Sierra shouting to her.

"Ambush!"

Tara heard Sierra unsheathe her blade, and with a delicate finesse, leapt down from the carriage and to her horse's side, pulling her shortsword from its holdings and raising it into a defensive stance as a gang of five men tried to surround them.

“I take this to be a common trick of yours?” Sierra asked of the men, her sword held firm, her stance an ebb more aggressive than Tara’s.

“It brings us a tidy sum, patrolsman” one of the men replied, recognising her armour as he weighed them up “Speaking of which, would you be so kind as to empty your pockets, so we might be on our way?”

Polite bandits; now Tara had seen everything.

“Not going to happen” Sierra spoke with strength “And if any of you try to take anything from us, none of you will leave here; this I promise you.”

Tara couldn’t help but admire her confidence; bandits may well be much the same across the land, but Orcish bandits were uniquely intimidating in their presence and reputation.

“Who are you to make threats to us?” one of the other bandits asked “We have you outnumbered!”

“And I have you outclassed. Now stand aside.”

A couple of the men fidgeted with their weapons.

“And what of your friend?” the first bandit asked, an edge closer now “Can she hold her own, cover your back?”

Sierra stayed quiet a moment too long.

“I thought not” the man smiled “Boys?”

With that they advanced on them, Sierra’s sword raising to meet her would-be attackers. But then she heard the fast swings of metal through air, and glanced quickly behind her; she saw Tara moving her sword with deft hands in a style she had never seen – a technique that was alien to her.

It made her wonder.

The men had stopped their advance, transfixed as Sierra was at Tara's unexpected display, before she then finished with a thrusting down-and-out movement to her side.

There was a pause, tense and silent.

"I have come from the front lines of the war with the Hamurfelions" Tara spoke loud, her nerves well hidden "Fighting alongside and against men and women bigger and stronger than any of you. You've just seen how I handle a blade. You can see my companion's armour. So, if it isn't obvious, let me tell you what these things mean: you should run."-the men looked doubtful, despite her display, but she continued none-theless-"Run and don't look back, for we will end you. I gift you this warning; try your hand against us and you will feel the sting of your final losses."

"In short lads, you think you're a danger to us? No, we're a danger to you" Sierra added, impressed by Tara's act of words "And for the record, we're only giving you the chance to walk away because we have a schedule to keep."

There was another, longer tense silence, the bandits eyeing one another as their leader made a decision, a slow breeze now pulling through from the south.

"You talk tough sister"' he said, lowing his weapon a near imperceptible amount "The both of you do, I respect that. Tell you what, your friend beats my man Oro here"-he pointed to a man head and shoulders taller than Tara, wielding an old rust-ed mace and fur pauldrons-"and we'll let you be on your way, *warrior.*"

"You expect me to trust that you'll keep your word?" Sierra probed, the thought of Tara having to fight unpleasant to her.

“I’m hurt” the bandit leader laughed “But I see your point – I wouldn’t trust me either. Lads?”-he gave a gesture with his hands, and his men sheathed their weapons and moved to the side-“See sister? I’m a man of my word.”

“I’ll fight instead” Sierra stated firmly.

“Not the deal, sister.”

“Take it or I end you first”-Sierra tightened her grip on her sword-“I win, we leave without a fuss; those are my terms.”

“Ha! You have one hell of a spine; you two a thing or somin’?”-Sierra gave him a look that could level mountains-“Fine, fine”-he held his hands high in a faux apology-“Oro, if you could oblige her?”

With that Oro leapt at her, Tara ducking back and out of the way of the slashing blade and thrashing metal, grasping hold of their horses’ reins quickly to prevent them from bolting at the sudden eruption of violence.

The bandits cheered as Oro forced Sierra to duck and back-step with almost every swing and strike.

Tara looked at Sierra, then to the horses, then the open road.

The bandits were distracted with the fight; she could run, leave Sierra behind to fight off the bandits alone and continue with her mission.

She looked back at Sierra.

She was still ducking and rolling from Oro’s attempts to rend her head from her shoulders.

Tara looked – glanced – at her easy means of escape; she rested a hand upon the hilt of her shortsword, and stayed.

As she watched, she noticed – beyond the jeering the bandits gave, laughing at what they saw as cowardice in Sierra’s moves

– that Sierra hadn't taken so much as a parrying swing at Oro, and realised that Sierra was waiting, watching how Oro moved, looking for the right moment.

"Fight, ya blooday coward!" Oro yelled at her; Sierra stayed quiet, sidestepping yet another would-be fatal blow with ease.

And then, as Oro went to follow up with a strong upwards strike, Sierra deftly slid her sword through Oro's underarm as she spun out of his way, driving it sideways through him to the hilt, pulling it back out of him with her momentum before stopping behind him.

The bandits went quiet.

Oro fell upon his face, his rusted mace clattering against the stone of the road.

Tara held her breath, waiting for the bandits to charge them in anger.

"Shit sister, I didn't think you'd actually kill him!" the leader yelled; then he laughed "But the bastard deserved it, I assure you" his grin was all teeth and ended at his eyes; it left Tara unnerved.

"I assume our deal stands?" Sierra asked, ready for it not to be.

"Sure, a deal's a deal; ain't gonna break my word just to lose more of my men to that dance-fighting of yours sister"-she couldn't tell if that was a compliment or an insult-"You sisters have safe travels now."

Needless to say, the two of them got as far away from there as fast as was possible.

*

They didn't stop riding until they came upon a walled town where Sierra said her fellow warriors would rest and resupply. Tara asked whether warriors going to the front stopped here, Sierra replying that she wasn't sure.

After Sierra reported the bandits to the town's guardsmen, they ended up at the stables, the half of it commandeered by the Orcish military, as dusk left the air with a dulling orange glow.

"Relia"-Sierra answered Tara's question about the town-"A once popular name on the Eastern Isles" she mused, brushing down her horse "Surprised you didn't come this way when you were going to the front."

"Yeah" Tara shrugged nonchalantly, passing her lack of knowledge off as a side-effect of her life's unusual travels "I moved out with a detachment of troops and supplies – arrows and the like"-Sierra raised an eyebrow-"Sorry, warriors" she smirked "We had to take the coastal roads for reasons that were not mine to know."

"Where in the Isles do they call warriors 'troops'?" Sierra asked, amused by the misphrasing.

"Up north, northeast" Tara lied, feeding an overripe apple to her horse; she had grown attached to the sturdy beast "Near the border with Bahvain" Tara hoped Sierra had never been there, else things could go very wrong, very fast.

"Haven't been up north" Sierra mused, patting her horse affectionately, her brushing done "What's it like?"

"Oh you know, mountainous in parts, flat in the valleys" she chuckled, turning to Sierra "You sure there's space for us in the barracks?"

"Should be; there's always one warrior stationed there – at least since the start of the war – and it's mostly just us on patrol duties that use it."

"Will we have any privacy?"

Sierra looked at her, a playful, cheeky look in her eyes.

"Why, what were you thinking of doing tonight?"

Tara gave a laugh.

"Seriously though Sierra, I'm a rather...private person"-Sierra moved to speak, but Tara continued over her-"I know we've been intimate, that I shared myself quite readily with you, but"-she paused, biting her lip as she looked for words to say-"I'm not saying it was a mistake – it wasn't, and it, you, were and are wonderful – but that's not who I am."-Sierra's eyes softened, hearing her, and not just her words-"That happened because I was in a vulnerable place; if it had been another time, another place..."

"I understand."

"Do you?" Tara questioned sincerely "I hope so, because...being with you...I like it. More than like it. I...I guess what I'm saying – what I'm asking of you – is to tread lightly, to treat me with care; intimacy is difficult for me – and not just the physical side – even telling you this is something of a struggle.

Sierra put down the horse brush she still held in her left hand upon a wooden stool that sat against the wall, and put her hands in Tara's.

"Thank you for trusting me then" she smiled "But, does this mean all the...*intimate* confidence, has that all been a lie?"

"I would nev-"-she caught herself before she could say it- "I...yes, no" Tara shrugged "I feel safe – happy – when I feel you against me, I feel home when your arms are wrapped around me. But words...telling you how I feel, telling you my whole truth, is...it's something that will take time, and patience on your part."

Sierra rubbed a thumb across the back of Tara's hand.

"A good thing we're on a fairly long journey then isn't it?"

Tara couldn't help but return the smile with which Sierra spoke, even if she was looking down at their entwined hands.

'This is silly' Tara thought 'How she makes me feel, makes me forget...it's like being a naïve girl again.'

She looked up at Sierra.

"You still haven't answered my question" she gave a wry grin "Will we have any privacy?"

"There are a few separate rooms we could use, if that would calm your soul."

Tara gave a nod to that, hesitating to ask what she wanted to ask a moment.

"Sierra" she began "Tonight, could...could we...cuddle?"

"You need ask?" Sierra replied, eyebrow raised "After what we've done together?"

"Maybe not, but I just...I would really, very much just like for you to hold me tight, to rest my head upon your chest and do nothing more than feel you against me – to feel your chest rise and fall with each breath, to feel the rhythm of your heartbeat."

"...Okay. I think I understand what you're asking" Sierra answered, reading beyond the words themselves "But I will ask of you one thing in return."

"Oh?"

Sierra leaned in, planting a kiss upon Tara's dark lips.

They stood there, embraced, for what felt like an eternity of the most pleasant kind.

"You know" Tara said after a moment once the kiss had ended, still lost in the feeling of butterflies in her chest "You probably need to have another go at that, just to be sure."

Sierra placed a hand upon Tara's face, running the tips of her fingers through Tara's hair intimately, and kissed her again.

CHAPTER THIRTEEN

Outskirts of Vilwood

Ji'Roh could not believe his eyes.

He did not want to believe his eyes.

He ran with all his might, for discovery now would mean certain death and put an end to Val'Ur's plans. He could feel tears fall from his eyes as he made for Bahvain, his horse left behind as it had been seen; better for it to be thought to belong to one of those poor souls than risk them realising their atrocities had been witnessed. It had been a massacre of the bloodiest form, such ruthlessness he could scarcely believe it to be real, let alone witnessed by his own eyes. He realised, of course, that

Kaymar had known about this; hence his warnings against taking the western road. He felt sick as his legs finally gave out from under him, forcing him to vomit at the images burned into his mind. He stayed on his knees a while, listening intently to see if he was being tracked; thankfully he could only hear the noise of crickets and grasshoppers in the nearby brush and the thunderous beating of his own heart.

Finally getting back to his feet, he continued onward, heading north towards the township of Bahvil, and then from there to Hamurfel. He knew Korren'Ur was bad, corrupt, from what Roselia had told him, but this? This was an act of a monster; but who was worse, the one who gave the order or the ones who followed it? He shook his head as he went for his hipflask, taking a much needed sup of water. He was not sure he would ever get that sight out of his head, but at least there was a witness to the atrocity, someone to vouch for those who had been slain. He was now even more determined – adamant and sure – that the King and True Queen of Hamurfel would aid them against this madman – despite the current hostilities between their two people – once they heard of this horror.

As the sun set, the moon obscured by cloud cover, Ji'Roh continued his forward march, unable and unwilling to sleep.

CHAPTER FOURTEEN

Near the Southern Coastal Road, Orcish lands

The wind lashed and whipped across them, the horses laying down against each other and the tree they were tied to, heads tucked low against themselves. Sierra held tight to Tara as they braced against what cover they could, the sound of a wind-toppled tree crashing to the ground quietly coming over the booming thrusts of the wind itself. Pressed between them was Tara's satchel and its precious cargo of letters; the pair were within the same bedroll, leaning hard against a small, cracked boulder that barely broke the wind as it fell against them. All that was making the windstorm bearable was the knowledge that it would eventually pass, and the comfort found in each other's arms.

Tara pressed her head against Sierra's collar, eyes closed and arms wrapped tightly around her, Sierra's head resting upon hers as she tried to keep Tara warm, their hair being blown uncontrollably.

Once the storm had passed, Sierra checked on the horses as Tara went over their supplies – checking and rechecking that the King's letter was still safely in her satchel.

"How they doing?" she asked as she offered Sierra a drink from one of the waterskins.

"A bit worse for wear, but okay all-in-all" Sierra replied, taking a swig from the waterskin "Hardy beasts those two; how's our supplies?"

"Mostly there – the letters are safe – but we lost all of our bread, bar a few crumbs."

"There goes any hope for toast in the morning" Sierra laughed, Tara smirking at her good humour "Surprised we didn't lose more though."

"Same; guess we were lucky – or as much as one can be whilst stuck in a storm." Tara shrugged, before asking a question as they moved to ready the horses "I didn't squeeze you too hard, did I?"

"Nah – I actually enjoyed holding you so close" Sierra replied with a wry smile "feeling your heart beat so close to mine felt...comforting."

Tara blushed.

"Well it felt nice to be kept safe in those strong arms of yours."

"They can do more than hold you, you know."

"Oh stop it you" Tara stuck her tongue out at her playfully, her guard dropped.

Sierra jumped up upon her faithful steed, waiting for Tara as she climbed upon hers.

"Ready?"-Tara gave a nod-"Right then; time we started going south."

They had rode for several mostly silent hours, taking a steady speed in the new heat that had replaced the windstorm from before, careful to not fatigue their horses in the Sun's inescapable glare. When they did break the silence, it was to stop for a break or to trade stories – Tara taking care to not be too specific or revealing with her own – until they began to approach, then pass, ruins of an old township that Tara found hard to gauge the age of.

"What is this place?" she asked, her eyes searching the overgrown stone and broken walls out of both curiosity and an incessant need to look out for any potential ambush.

"Havengrowth" Sierra's tone became uncharacteristically sombre, much to Tara's intrigue "A place all warriors learn of when we first begin our training."

"What happened to it?"

Sierra was slow to answer, her gaze unshifting from the ruins as they continued passing it by.

"It was butchered" she said at last, pulling herself away from it so she might look at Tara as she spoke "It is a...a horrifying tale, one that is largely kept from civilians"-Tara could tell she didn't want to tell her the tale, which said quite a lot-"I – do you really want to know? I wouldn't want to bore you."

"I don't think you could ever bore me – you're far too interesting" Tara smiled without meaning to, her cheeks going quite red as she caught how sweetly she had said it.

Sierra smirked a small grin at that.

"Still" Sierra began again, looking back to the ruins "the lesson – the point of them teaching every new class of warriors about this place – is about never underestimating your foe, or hesitating in the heat of battle...that's something of an over-simplification, but..." she trailed off, unsure of how to end the sentence; she was more used to and comfortable with speaking of less troubling things.

"It's okay not to tell me, you know, if it makes you feel uncomfortable" Tara patted her on the shoulder, having pulled her horse closer to Sierra's.

Sierra gave a thankful smile, and they continued in silence a while, taking in the eerie quiet of the ruins.

The pair finally passed the last ruined wall of Havengrowth, and continued onward, soon forgetting its small part in their journey. Had they been travelling in the other direction, however, they would have noticed a small cairn, with an aged slab of stone behind it, weathered and covered in lichen; if one were to look close upon it and study its faded words, all that could be discerned would have been:

'Charl- - -, Da-ght-r of Dr—rix'

***

The two lay next to one another, kissing gently if passionately, arms woven around each other.

They had found a small tavern along the southern road they now travelled to Yarmor – a port town where ferries would go to and from the mainland to the Orc Isles themselves – and had used some of Sierra's coin to rent a room for the night, and buy them each a warm bowl of stew; a nice change from storm-lost bread and stale crackers, and sleeping out in the open for that matter.

"Sierra"-Tara pulled back from their embrace a little; just enough to look Sierra in the eye-"forgive how this question may sound, but can...can I trust you?"

Sierra's eyes looked at her softly.

"I could ask the same of you, but here we are"-she twirled the base of Tara's hair – something that was, unbeknownst to her, a most intimate thing Tara would let no-one else do-"I get that we are, despite our time together, still new to each other – at least in certain ways. Perhaps that is what has drawn us so close so fast."

"The novelty of each other?" Tara asked, and Sierra was sure she sounded hurt by the implication.

"Not quite what I meant." Sierra reassured her "But to answer your question: yes, you can trust me, for I'm trusting you – not just with my body, but with my heart, with my...hope."

Tara blushed; something she had noticed herself doing a lot lately.

"That's awfully poetic and sweet for a warrior" Tara smiled wryly.

"What can I say, I'm a romantic"-she nuzzled the end of Tara's nose with hers-"And if I may be frank and open, I sense something good about you Tara, something worth exploring and getting to know."

Tara stayed quiet; she had fallen for this Orcish girl, despite her efforts – however half-hearted they may have been – and that was likely to cause her problems. It worried her, in more ways than one, but isn't she deserving of love? Can't she too have – find – happiness as the True Queen and Lady Ur had? But...she was loyal to her King, to Hamurfel, to her people; she had given her word to see her mission through, no matter the cost.

"Tara?" Sierra cajoled her "Where'd you go?"

"Oh, I was just thinking."

"About?"

"You" Tara smiled, unable to lie, not able to tell the whole truth.

"Oh? Do tell" Sierra snuggled closer.

"Those eyes of yours sure are beautiful" Tara sighed, avoiding the question "I could get lost in them for days on end without regret."

"You flatter me."

"It's true"-she gave a quiet yawn, resting her head lightly against Sierra's-"So, how far do we have to go tomorrow?"

"Well, o' messenger mine, if we leave early and the weather holds, we could make it halfway to Yarmor."

"Best we get some sleep then."

"Aye, my love."

"...did, did you just call me your 'love'?"

Sierra opened her eyes.

"Too soon?" she asked, worried she may have overstepped in her tired state.

Tara thought on it, her heart giving a small pang at those thoughts.

"No...strangely, I think"-she kissed Sierra on the forehead-"I think it was just the right moment."

CHAPTER FIFTEEN

South Bahvain halfway between the Orcish Border and Bahvil Town

Ji'Roh crept through the rough brush, carefully as to not spook the herd of sickleback that grazed upon the bulbous tubers that naturally grew in the area with abundance. He held his breath as he eyed up their tusks; they looked sharp enough to warrant a healthy dose of fear.

He had barely slept since witnessing the horrors at Vilwood, in part from the nightmares that came from it, in part his determination to reach the Hamurfelion court as soon as possible so that they might know the truth. There was another determination though, another reason to march on outside his duty to Val'Ur; his dear Roselia. His heart burned with his missing of her, and the possibility that she could be with child. She was not a hundred percent sure she was before he left, but all indications were there, and by now she would know, and he had hope that she were.

His thoughts returned abruptly to his current predicament as he pushed through a wall of leaves, finding a young, juvenile sickleback that stared at him. In a moment of startled panic, he tried to back away, a twig snapping underfoot loudly as he did.

It began calling for its mother.

Distressful calls.

Ji'Roh ran before he heard the aggressive stomping and squealing of the mother, and the other members of the herd.

He did not look back. There was no need; he could hear them charging.

He could hear them snap and push through all the bushes and saplings he had been dodging.

He thought on how well things would go if he tried to fend them off; he quickly threw that idea away.

A shallow ravine, there was a shallow ravine coming up on his left.

He glanced over, judging his chances; there was a stream running through its centre, and few rocks to break himself upon by the looks of things.

The sickleback herd was getting closer now they were in a clearer area.

He dove into the ravine's sloped sides, tucking his head beneath his arms as he tumbled towards the stream, hoping he would miss the rocks, and the sickleback would have enough sense to not chase after him.

CHAPTER SIXTEEN

Palace of the Dred King, Hamurfel, Akiro Region

The Dred King paced angrily around his throne, a nervous servant standing to the side awaiting any commands that could be shouted at him. The King was waiting on a highly respected duo of physicians from Blackwood – John Kalib and Samara Prime – whom he had summoned to treat his sister, the True Queen, who's condition had begun to worsen; his court physicians – despite their whole hearted efforts – were at a loss as to how to treat her, and thus had felt his rage – though they were only harmed emotionally.

What enraged him further was the seemingly unending war with the Orcs. He took each soldier's death, each maiming, as a personal blow – not that he would show it – and furthermore, it was that it caused such heartache as he was forced to lie to his sister about her beloved's absence every time she would ask, and the pained look on her face that they were still apart.

'Damn that Chancellor' he thought to himself, nigh on screaming inside his head 'I swear I shall carve out his heart for this! What end is he after? What cost of death will be too high?'

His thoughts were interrupted by the sound of the far door opening, three cloaked individuals, sand coating them like fine dust on the furniture of a forgotten room, entering the throne room as he took his seat.

"My King" the first bellowed as the other two unwrapped their faces "I present to you the doctors from Blackwood" he gave a ceremonial bow as he pointed to his companions.

The King regarded them quietly, taking a moment to weigh them up before beckoning them closer.

"You are Kalib and Samara, yes?" he asked.

"Indeed we are, your highness" Kalib replied politely "Your summons mentioned a delicate health matter?"

The King turned his gaze to his emissary, who gave a silent nod in assurance of their identity.

"Indeed"-he rose from his throne-"Follow me...I trust you have your medical necessities?"

"We believe so your highness; your writ was quite vague – which we understand is for your privacy – so we had to bring a wide range of supplies" Samara answered as they followed him.

"They are in the coach we arrived in" Kalib added.

“I shall have them brought to you” the King said dryly, gesturing for his servant to do so.

They walked in silence as he led them towards his sister’s room, Samara and Kalib exchanging glances that were equal parts nervousness and excitement at working for the Hamurfelion royalty. As the Dred King went to open the door he stopped, glancing back at the pair of them.

“Your patient is in this room; my sister – the True Queen Amira – to whom I expect you to show the proper respect” his tone was dry and serious.

“Of course sir.”

“...She is very delicate, fragile, so do not act unthinkingly, nor repeat what I have said to her. And, I cannot stress this enough, DO NOT tell her, nor mention, the war with the Orc Isles. Is that understood?”

“I assure you Dred King, our only concern is giving her the treatment she requires, our only interactions shall be confined to such.” Samara said confidently and reassuringly.

“Not a word of war shall pass our lips, we give you our word on that” Kalib assured him also.

He nodded silently, then opened the door and led them inside.

“Amira, I have brought you new doctors to look over you with fresh eyes” he smiled, his mannerisms and tone of voice noticeably gentler and softer in her presence.

“Oh brother, your kindness is so sweet, but I feel like such a bother to you” she gave a weak smile, her left arm jolting in a sudden spasm; a symptom of her illness that had begun as a near unnoticeable twitch.

"No bother at all dear sister, just doing what I can to make you better."

As the pair of physicians talked to her about how she felt, and looked her over, the Dred King stood at the back of the room, watching anxiously as his thoughts turned to Nor'un's plan, his desperation for the war to be over blinding him to the real threat ahead of him.

CHAPTER SEVENTEEN

Ebo, Orc Isles

Val'Ur crushed the blue powder block into the concave disc, adding the tiniest drop of water as she pressed it out with her stone pestle. Alongside this were a few other discs, all the same size, some with uncrushed colour blocks, others already made into a paste like dust. She picked up a thick, smooth brush, lightly dabbing it into the disc of black paste that had been waiting next to the blue one, lifting it to her eyes and began to paint. She drew undershadows, pulling the brush across from her nose and arching down slightly at her ears, then wiping lightly with a washcloth at a few imperfections and readying her next brush as she looked at herself in her mirror.

She turned her head, thinking on how Amira would probably tell her she'd put too much effort into her face-paint whilst also swooning over it; it made her smile, if only briefly.

She used a finer, medium sized brush that was a little wider than the others to paint the blue, half overlapping over the black beneath her eyes. She added a twirl that came over her brow, drawing up from her nose; it was something new, far more fanciful than her usual style, and as such felt that she would need Roselia's opinion on it. She checked her face in the mirror, looking to see if she had managed to keep the symmetry of the paint 'just so', noticing how much more vibrant her own eyes seemed now they were bounded by colour and shadow.

Amira was a gentle soul, a gentle heart that was easy to love, and Roselia was much the same – in a distinctly Orcish way. Val'Ur was very thankful to be able to call her her friend, especially in the here-and-now. They had taken to sharing Val'Ur's bed, each comforted by the other's friendly embrace in the dark of night; both of their lovers were far from them, across battle lines of a war that should never have been.

It hurt her heart, having to spend all this time and distance from Amira, from her wife-to-be.

What worried her most was Amira's health; she had been so fragile when she had last seen her, and though she had wanted to stay, her father had recalled her to the Isles under the guise of an emergency. She realised too late that the 'emergency' was her father's war with the Hamurfelions.

Now she was using a finer, puffier brush and a dusting sponge to apply the white paint, almost sold in some parts, ghostly dusting that faded away in others.

She remembered how she had first met Amira, then their first days of courtship. She had fallen for her almost in an instant, or so it had felt, in all the obvious ways. But her love for her? That had grown – grew stronger and stronger – as she watched her and learned who she was in her heart-of-hearts; it was how she treated others, both in action and words, and the kind thoughts she put towards her people.

She remembered being shown the Royal Tombs – a sacred thing for Amira to do – and Amira telling her of the tales of her ancestors, and eventually of her father as they came to his tomb. Orcs and Hamurfelions couldn't get more different in seemingly uncountable ways – according to some at least – but Amira had a way of finding commonalities between people; it was a gift of hers, a gift with words and how to weave them.

Roselia entered the room, Val'Ur looking over her face-paint intently in her mirror.

"He's asking for you again" Roselia told her, rubbing her growing belly absently as she did "I told him you had duties to attend to."

Val'Ur smiled a 'thank you' as Roselia tended to some potted flowers Val'Ur had brought back from Hamurfel years ago.

"Rose" Val'Ur asked, still facing her mirror "What do you think of this?" she pointed to the blue twirls that landscaped the space above her brow.

Roselia cocked her head, setting down a mug of water she had been using to water the flowers.

"It's different."

"Is that a good different, or a bad different?"

"A 'different' different" Roselia chimed, pulling up a stool to sit on next to Val'Ur "Why the change anyway?"

Face-paint in Orcish society was a complex thing. For some it was ceremonial, rarely worn. For others, there would not be a day where it was not worn; it all depended on the Isle one grew up on, with the odd exception born of masonry custom. Then came the meaning of the face-paint, portrayed through the colours and patterns used, the layerings and techniques. What was true – universally so – was that it was sacred, and a means by which to show one's true self in a way words are rarely capable.

"I feel...when I see Amira again, I wish, I would like for her to see how I've changed, but also that our love – my love for her – has remained an everlasting constant."

Roselia put an arm around Val'Ur's.

"Well, I think if you feel that it shows that, then it does."

"But I must be sure, Rose"-she paused-"Perhaps I should stick to my normal face-paint..."

"Or" Roselia suggested, looking over the flow of colour upon Val'Ur's face "You could keep this style for something special – like when you see Queen Amira again – and use your usual style for everything else?"

"Perhaps" Val'Ur looked at the curved, faded edges upon her face "But I think Amira...I would enjoy her opinion about now."

"Hopefully Ji'Roh will be delivering your message as we speak Val" Roselia sighed wistfully "And you and Amira will be reunited by the end of this month, or the next."

"I admire your positivity, however unlikely it seems to me."

Val'Ur lightly tapped a finger into her white paint, wiping off the excess on its disc's edge, before then misting out the harsher edges of her blue twirls as Roselia watched.

"You know Val, for a lady of stone, you don't half have a soft touch."

Val'Ur almost smudged her face-paint as she laughed.

"Don't make me blush" she smirked, before wiping her hand on her washcloth "...Do you know how long...no, never mind."

Roselia got to her feet, lightly patting Val'Ur on the shoulder, before fetching her a dram of whiskey.

"A bit early for that isn't it?"

"You're saying you don't want it?"

"That's not what I said" Val'Ur took the goblet in hand "Rose, I...thank you."

"You don't need to thank me my friend."

"But you have been so strong, and whilst in such a vulnerable state."

"There is more than one way to be strong, more than one way to be vulnerable" Roselia mused aloud, retaking her seat "I just wish I had been there when...when it happened."

Val'Ur stayed quiet, looking intently at her own face, her own eyes staring back at her from the mirror as if trying to tell herself something.

"What's on today's schedule?" she asked after a minute or two, thinking that the twirls were perhaps a bit too flamboyant for her own taste.

"There's a representative from the Western Isles – Iciro specifically – and a rally for returning warriors in the evening."

"How many returning this time?" she asked.

"Forty-four."

Val'Ur winced at the number; only the heavily wounded would be sent back from battle, most likely maimed and missing limbs. And that was nothing compared to the dead they represented.

"This war can't end soon enough"-she got to her feet, Roselia joining her, fetching her her formal overcoat-"Who's the representative?" Val'Ur asked as they left her room and Roselia locked the door behind them.

"A newish figure, Kori'Rhn, who hails from Iciro's largest fisher family."

"Is her visit related to the war?"

"No, it is regarding an expansion of their sea port and their fishing territories.

Val'Ur was relieved for the chance of such a distraction.

"Val?"

"Hm?"

"You look beautiful."

Val'Ur blushed with a smile she tried to hide, feeling a tad more confident for that.

***

She stood looking out of the stained-glass window of the Council Chamber, watching her people move and live. There had just been a meeting of the Lords and her father, its discussions dominated by war plans and associated supply lines. Messages going to and from the front lines were inconsistent in their timing – a side effect of the distance, terrain and bandits along the way that took advantage of the situation – and as such most of the time was spent arguing over what information to act upon, and which to ignore.

She watched a baker carry a basket of bread loaves up the steps below, her thoughts turning to how they were before the war – more constructive, even in their disagreements, less argumentative and more...just; even if it was only in appearance – biting at her lip as she pondered who she could trust.

The meeting had ended some minutes ago, and now she stood alone in the room, save for her ceremonial blade; her father had agreed to another meeting on the morrow, when they had all had a chance to calm down and rethink their approach.

She did not trust him. She hadn't for a long time.

She felt the hilt of her mighty blade, tied close to her hip in its sheath. It had been her mother's blade, and her grandfather's before her; she did not normally carry it – wear it upon her person – outside of ceremonies and formal meetings of the most important emissaries from across the land – normally it hung upon the wall adjacent to her bed, so she might keep that last part of her mother close, safe – but now was different. She remembered the stories her mother and grandfather would tell her, of how the sword was forged from the *Shadows* themselves, made to keep the truest loves safe in the Dark of their final hour; she still did not understand what they had meant, but it made her feel safe.

And after what had almost happened – what had happened – that was all she could ask for.

The great metal doors opened, and she turned to see who it was.

"Val'Ur, m'lady" Roselia greeted her formally, knowing their conversation would likely be overheard.

"Roselia" Val'Ur gave a soft smile, her hand no longer resting upon her sword's hilt.

"Lord Tallon's son requested your presence at this evening's meal"-Val'Ur's dismay shown only through her eyes, but very clearly so-"But I informed him you had other arrangements that were made far in advance; a fact I repeated firmly as he voiced his...displeasure."

Val'Ur walked over to her friend and handmaid, giving her a silent thankyou before they left the chamber together.

***

Val'Ur held her ear to Roselia's belly, intently listening to the new life that grew within. It was still a marvel to her, what their bodies were capable of.

"Have you thought of a name?" she asked as she returned to sitting upright.

"Not yet" Roselia smiled "Once Ji'Roh returns to us, then we will decide together."

"Makes sense" Val'Ur chewed at the side of her mouth in thought "Rose...about Ji'Roh, sending him-"

"I appreciate your concern, I really do" Roselia interrupted with a kind smile, placing a hand upon Val'Ur's "But there is no-one else I would have trusted with your message"-she gave a slight pause as she felt movement in her belly-"I love you my friend, and as such so does Ji'Roh; there is little he would not do for you."

Val'Ur put her other hand atop Roselia's.

"And I love you in kind. But I should not have put you in that situation, especially because I love you both; if you lose him I will never forgive myself."

Roselia tilted her head, thoughts upon how good a friend Val'Ur was, how it did not matter to her that she and Ji'Roh were not noble-born.

"You honour us" she said with a sincerity and warmth that shone deep into her voice "But Ji'Roh is brave and enduring; he'll make it back to us."

Val'Ur nodded with a smile.

"So" Roselia said with a tired sigh, looking at the glowing dim of sunlight as she changed the subject "What comes after?"

"After?"

"When we have peace, what will you and Amira do once you are married?"

Val'Ur thought on that as she put an arm around Roselia, letting her lean against her a little; she hadn't much considered that, least not since she had been recalled to Orcain. Her focus – outside of the more immediate concern of avoiding her father's trappings – had been on whether her plan succeeded, and what she would do if it failed.

"I'm not sure, perhaps...perhaps, if Amira wants it, we will have a child – when she is well enough."

"You have no interest in carrying a child yourself?" there was no judgment in her voice as she asked, just curiosity.

“I don’t want any man near me like that”-she shrugged her serious tone off with a brief, forced laugh-“No matter how good of a suiter he may be.”

“Hmm” Roselia pondered “I can but only imagine what it must be like – as you can tell, I have no such problem”-she gave an infectious laugh as she gestured to her abdomen-“But it is what is needed for a child, so it is.”

“Aye.”

“Did you have someone in mind?”

“We haven’t – hadn’t – had chance to discuss it before the war.”-There was a pause, and Roselia could hear the tears in her voice as she looked down at her hands-“I just miss her so much...”

Roselia knew quite well that beneath her stone-hard exterior, Val’s heart was as soft and caring as any other.

“Oh Val...” she said, moving to comfort her.

“It’s...it’s okay, it’s just hard sometimes.”

There came a knocking at her chamber door; politely spaced rapping against the stone that was emblematic of a Palace servant. Roselia got up from her seat and saw to it as Val'Ur took the moment to fetch herself the last of her Iciron whiskey.

“Anything important?” she asked as Roselia closed and relocked the door, sipping at her peaty drink with a little fervour.

“Just a letter” she replied, Val'Ur gesturing her to open it “Dearest Val, thank you for your gift...”-Roselia began to read, stopping as she quietly read ahead, having seen Ji’Roh’s name be mentioned-“Val, this is from Kaymar.”

Val'Ur lowered her glass, looking at her with nervous expectancy.

"Well?"

"He writes much to obfuscate his answer from prying eyes" she replied, handing Val'Ur the letter "But I assume you can make it out?"

Val was quiet a moment as she read, a smile drawing itself upon her lips.

"He will give us his aid" she looked up at Rose, relief clear and glowing in her expression.

"What of Ji'Roh? I saw his name mentioned but I dared not interpret Kaymar's words."

"He is fine, at least when Kaymar wrote this" she said, looking back to the words and their double meaning "Headed for Hamurfel as we speak..."

"What is it Val?" Roselia asked, seeing her friend's brow furrow at something.

"I'm not sure, something about his tone here is off, like he is trying to apologise about something...I think he thinks I know something I don't."

"Like what?"

"I...I'm not sure" she near murmured, thumbing the paper absently "but I fear it will end up being some machination of my father."

"Well whatever it is, we'll face it together."

Val'Ur looked up at her, her eyes drifting across her friend with a smile.

"Sometimes, Rose, I think you are the strongest person I know."

"Only sometime?" Roselia joked.

CHAPTER EIGHTEEN

Southern Coastal Road
Orcish Lands

They were not far from Yarmor, where they would take a ferry to Orcain, perhaps another day's ride, a day-and-a-half at most. The road was busier now – unsurprising for where they were – with traders and travellers of all kinds passing by in either direction, and Sierra was humming a soft tune.

Tara listened attentively to the melody – the rise and fall of the notes – wondering if it belonged to a song or simply something Sierra was inventing in the moment. The sun, whilst warming, was dulled slightly by an overcast weave of clouds that left the landscape bathed in tolerable light and a gentle, caressing breeze that ebbed and flowed.

The landscape wasn't barren, nor overgrown wilds, but a patchwork of small, managed woods, clutches of small houses that could barely pass as villages – most were too small even for that – that occupied the space between farmlands; there was no mistaking this as one of the mainstays of the Orc Isle's food supply.

Tara remarked on how they balanced their industrious needs for food and the natural wilderness that surrounded them, and Sierra laughed.

"Isn't that true of all Orcs?" she smiled.

"Yes, but it still amazes me"-Tara felt even the mild deception in her words cutting to herself-"I have seen folk from afar bring ruin to themselves in their hunger, blinded by ambition and greed."

"I have heard of such things" Sierra nodded "They are few – those who lack the knowledge to respect from whence we came. Besides, the wilds bring us sustenance; it is only right we return the favour with respect and reverence."

"Well said."

Tara looked over at her lover – lover; she had never thought she would call another that again – hoping for-

"Tara"-Sierra interrupted her thoughts-"way back, when those bandits tried to ambush us?"

"And you showed them it was best to walk away?" Tara grinned "What about it?"

"Where did you learn to wield your sword like that?"

If Tara had been her usual self – the elite messenger unmatched in her espionage and stealth – she would have noticed there was more than curiosity in Sierra's tone; but alas, in the here-and-now, she was all too focused on how she wanted things to be.

"Oh that? Just something I picked up at the front – watching warriors and the like – not that there's any real substance behind it; my combat skills are only the basics I'm afraid."

"Hmm" Sierra raised an eyebrow "and here's me thinking you could teach me a thing or two."

"Who said I couldn't show you a thing or two?" Tara smirked humorously, like one does when flirting around someone who makes them feel safe.

"Oh really?" Sierra chuckled "We'll see."

The two continued onward, horses calmly trotting at a steady pace underfoot, until, a little while later, Sierra began humming again.

Tara found herself humming along to her tune.

CHAPTER NINETEEN

Yarmor, East Sojourn, Orcish lands

Tara could taste the salt in the air as they waited for the evening ferry. The sea breeze was oddly warm as it wafted in from the south, the sight of Orcain and its monolithic mountains – where Orc Isles Peak, home of the capital city of Ebo, was situated – towering upon the horizon. She stared at it solemnly, one hand firmly on her sealed pouch, her thoughts going over plans and contingencies for getting in – and out – of the Chancellor's Palace (and if the chance presented itself, the chambers of the Orcish Lords).

Sierra gave her a little nudge, breaking her out of her thoughts, and handing her a pastry she had bought from a storefront up the pier.

"Thanks" she whispered quietly as Sierra checked over their horses.

As she ate, Tara looked at her silently as seagulls called to each other in the background; she felt a deep sense of unease about her, conflicted by feelings of worry as to her fate when all was said and done. Sierra had let her hair down, her helm left on the bench beside Tara, her Orcish patrol armour lightly glinting in the sun's rays despite having dulled over time and use, the symbolled cloth that hung over the lightmail visibly worn, yet still looking well kept. Tara found her beautiful, which initially had come as a surprise to herself; her medium length, light brown hair and a somewhat pale complexion, and being a bit shorter than her, not being her usual type at all. It was a worry for her, as it made her mission substantially more complicated and dangerous, but she would not readily abandon this second chance at happiness.

Around them were a generous number of travellers for that time of day, each individual, group and family having looks of anxiousness, excitement and blissful indifference towards their travel to Orcain, the main isle of the Orc Isles, each with their own reasons; some returning home, some on business – perhaps there were some sightseers among them too. Tara regarded them with a sigh, finding their innocence – or naivety – rather symbolic of the whole conflict their two peoples were engaged in; 'Do they even know why they were at war?' she wondered silently.

"You're looking serious" Sierra quipped as she sat down beside her.

"Just thinking of home" she replied absently "and hoping this wind doesn't take any of these letters."

"Oh? You know, you've never told me where that was these days" Sierra asked expectantly, before noticing Tara's mind was still somewhere else, far away "Ah, the ferry's coming in" she pointed to the ship, now highly visible, and just under a third of a league out.

Tara nodded silently, a small gust coming up the pier as she did.

"I do love the smell of the sea" Sierra said, once again trying to start a conversation.

"Sierra...just...sea travel makes me uneasy, that's all" Tara lied, sensing her unsaid question.

"Anything else?"

Tara gave a stern look that told her to leave it be.

"Fine"-Sierra rolled her eyes, exasperated-"Actually, no, no it's not fine; one minute we're all close and intimate, the next you're cold as ice, what is going on with you?"

Tara bit her lip.

"Just leave it, okay?"

"Why should I?"

"Because you're still practically a stranger to me! We've known each other, what, a little over two months? You have no place-"

"Don't. You. Dare." Sierra fumed "After all you've told me, after how intimate we've been, that's your excuse? That we're strangers, that I have no place to speak?!"-she gave an frustrated sigh-"I care about – I love you, okay? And I can see something's troubling you, so...please let me in."

They stared at each other a moment, the squawks of seagulls filling the silence between them as they flew overhead, a lone cloud drifting by.

Tara took a deep breath, and took hold of one of Sierra's hands.

"I...I'm sorry. I've been getting myself worked up over my duties, and what we have between us scares me – it scares me to be vulnerable with someone – and I've been taking it out on you, and I apologise" Tara said truthfully without the full truth.

Sierra's expression softened.

"Thank you; apology accepted" she put her arms around her "It's okay to be scared, after all you've lost, but you need not fear being vulnerable around me; I can keep you safe" she went in for a kiss, but Tara gently pushed her back.

"Sierra, I am no simple messenger."

"I figured" Sierra interrupted "The way you act around that pouch of yours, and the fact you've come from the front lines, it stands to reason you'd have more than messages for the warriors' families."

"I can't tell you what...what I'm delivering, but I do not want to keep secrets from you; I want this – us – to work out" Tara said, eyes glistening, as she barely held herself back from telling Sierra her secret.

"I understand" Sierra smiled "We all have our duties to uphold."

Tara glanced over at the ferry, now only a few short minutes from coming alongside the pier.

"Won't be long 'till we're at the capital" she sighed, before then returning her gaze to Sierra "I would like us to take it slow – between us that is – after I've made my deliveries."

"A bit late for that isn't it?" Sierra laughed in an attempt to alleviate the tension of the past few moments.

"You know what I mean" Tara chuckled, before then planting a quick kiss upon her lips.

"What was that for?"

"Because you're cute" she smiled "Now, we should probably bring the horses over so we're ready to board."

As Sierra began untying the horses from their post, smiling happily as she did, Tara worried to herself about whether her allegiance to the King would cost her something far more precious, the words 'I love you' still loud in her ears.

CHAPTER TWENTY

Chancellor's Palace
Ebo, Orcain

Roselia walked up the hallway towards Val'Ur's room, carrying a tray of unskinned fruits, cut bread and fresh butter; there was no need to bring a drink – Val'Ur's cabinet held enough for an army.

It would have been a lie to say she wasn't worried about Ji'Roh, or that the thought of raising their child without him didn't give her a cold chill, but she had faith in him. He was strong-willed – always had been, even as a child, when they first had met – and his love for her gave him all the power he needed, or so he would tell her. They had been together so long, and friends before even that, that that she had not heard his voice in so long, not seen his face...it could break a person; not Roselia though, she held to hope in a way few could.

She knocked upon Val'Ur's door.

"Lady Val" she called, cautious of being informal as one of the Palace's many servants walked by "I've brought you your lunch."

"Come in" Val'Ur answered, though she sounded distracted.

"...can, can I get you to open the door?" Roselia whispered through the door.

Val'Ur got up from her prone position upon her bed, walking briskly over to the door and opening it.

"Sorry Rose; how's the bump?"

"Growing larger by the day, or so it feels" Roselia chimed as she placed the tray upon Val's desk, before turning to her, rubbing a hand upon her belly "Want to feel?"

Val'Ur gingerly placed a hand upon her.

"Have you felt them kick?"

"I think it's too soon for that" Roselia replied, smiling down at her belly, then looking back up at Val'Ur "How was Kromahr?"

Val'Ur sighed.

"That bad?"

"No, no, Kromahr is fine. The people are fine, the port is well maintained, we've a steady stream of supplies coming in and going out."

"But?"

"Our officials are so...tiresome" Val'Ur took a seat at her desk as Roselia looked through Val's drinks cabinet for something appropriate to pair with her meal "You'd think everyone were a Hamurfelion spy the way they go on."

"I imagine they were trying to impress you with their thoroughness, however tiring they were to listen to"-Roselia brought over a light wine from Orura, one of the smaller Isles-"But I also imagine your presence boosted their morale too."

"Aye"-she gave Roselia a smile as she accepted her drink, now neatly poured into a silver goblet-"Though I'm half sure father thought I would have tried to escape on one of the ferries."-she gave a laugh, then sipped her wine-"I haven't had much time to talk since my return; any news from around Ebo?"

Roselia went quiet as she buttered a slice of bread whilst Val'Ur cut open one of the fruits.

"Tallon's son is back in the city" she answered at last, and Val almost froze in place, even if for the briefest of moments.

"I see" she ran her tongue along the front of her top teeth as she thought, Rose offering the now butter-lathered bread slice to her "Is he staying for long?"

"That I do not know"-Val took the bread, wrapping it around the soft yellow flesh of the fruit-"but I know he is boasting about chasing off some Hamurfelions from the north."

Val'Ur almost choked.

"From the north?"-Roselia gave a shrug-"Do people actually believe his lies?"

"More than you'd like Val, more than you'd like."

Val'Ur chewed, thinking silently as she enjoyed the flavour of her meal.

"Rose"-she began, having swallowed her mouthful-"I would appreciate it if my schedule did not align with his whilst he is here."

"Tallon's son?"

"Aye."

Rose began to butter another slice of bread, Val breaking open another, more stubborn fruit.

"Do you think he will pester me?" she asked after a moment of silence "I could really do without him and his...*ideas*."

"Not if I can help it m'lady"-she pulled a corner off the bread-"I do not understand what your father was thinking, forcing you into accepting his proposal."

"I know he's up to something Rose, why else butter up Tallon so?"

"'Butter up'?" Roselia laughed "Sorry Val, but you had to have said that on purpose."

Val'Ur gave a smile; she could always rely on her friend to cheer her up.

"Seriously though, you sure you can keep that creep away from me?"

"You have my word Val; after what you told me of him, there's no excuse I won't give to keep him at arm's length" she replied, patting Val'Ur upon the shoulder as she ate her torn piece of buttered bread.

"...I assume you're going to use your bump as an excuse for eating my lunch?" Val'Ur chuckled.

“Aye” Roselia licked a bit of butter off her finger “I am eating for two after all.”

CHAPTER TWENTY-ONE

The Ferry to Orcain, Orcish Sea

Tara stood next to Sierra, leaning upon the ferry's guard rail as they watched the sea race by; there was the faint sound of oars smacking against the light waves as they propelled them towards Orcain beneath the rumble of the other passengers' voices.

As they watched a small flock of seagulls trailing alongside the ferry, they talked about many things, some little and insignificant, others a little more personal and affecting. As they finished talking on some of their differences in opinion, Sierra lightly held Tara's hand, caressing it with her own.

"...I love how soft your hands are" she smiled absently.

Tara laughed.

"I had always thought them rough."

"Huh; perhaps it's just my soldier's hands then."

"Speaking of which, if...if you don't mind my asking, what do you think of the war?"

Sierra raised a questioning eyebrow.

"I sense there is more to that question then you're letting on."

"It's just, once I've finished my business in Ebo, your orders are to return to your patrol; I worry you'll be sent to the front lines."

"I see" Sierra looked down at the waves beneath them "I would like to say I'd give it up, that I'd walk away and settle down with you, find some other work, but warriors blood flows through my veins. I swore an oath to safeguard the Orc Isles and its people – no matter my feeling on the conflict – and I cannot simply walk away from that." Tara thought she sensed doubt in her voice, but then perhaps she was imaging it

They stood in silence a moment, listening to the sloshing waves.

"I hope you know how difficult this is for me Sierra, and I hope you understand, understand how much effort it takes to be myself – to be vulnerable – around you."

"I have noticed."

"Have you?"

"Yes" she gently squeezed Tara's hand "You've said it numerous times, and I am so thankful that you...that you allow yourself to be yourself around me, because I've found someone I truly care for, someone I can trust with my heart; so thank you

Tara for entrusting me with yours, and I swear to you, now and forever, that I shall never betray, take advantage of or take it for granted."

Tara gave her a kiss in response.

"Thank you" she whispered, Sierra smiling back in response "I…I needed to hear that."

They spent the next few minutes in silence as they drew closer to the port on Orcain's north-eastern side, the sun now a deep orange, a sole translucent cloud wafting just in front of its upper half as the sea breeze calmed almost to stillness as they leant against one another. Tara turned her head to look at Sierra, the orange rays lighting the side of her face, her left green eye illuminated, her right blue one reflecting the sea; it was a perfect moment.

"Marry me" Tara proclaimed softly as the other passengers scurried about to secure their luggage and animals for their arrival at the port in a few minutes time.

"…what?" Sierra responded with a nervous, quiet laugh, taken aback by this sudden question.

"Marry me" she asked once more, now holding both of Sierra's hands in hers "I love you; so let us marry, and damn the consequences." She could feel her heart flutter as she awaited Sierra's response.

"I…I, err…what happened to taking things slow?"

"Arrival in four minutes!" called a crewman as he walked the deck, interrupting Sierra's fumbling answer.

"Well?" Tara asked nervously as she felt her heart trying to fly away with her stomach.

"I...I should check on the horses, make sure they're ready for when we arrive."

Sierra went to walk away.

"Wait..." Tara grasped hold of her arm desperately.

"I just...I just need a moment; don't fret I...just, just a moment...okay?"

Tara turned away, looking down at her feet, then at the sea below, her eyes tearing up as Sierra walked away.

'Why Tara?' she thought to herself as the tears rolled down her cheek 'why'd you have to fall for her, only to chase her away?' she held her face in her hands as she wiped away at her tears.

Sierra stopped halfway across the ferry's deck, biting at her lip, her right hand tapping against her thigh anxiously. She turned, looking back at Tara; she was looking out to sea, but clearly crying. She looked away, thinking hard as her heart pounded harder than it ever had in any fight or skirmish.

She turned back to Tara.

"I'm sorry...I just panicked" Sierra called out as she strode back to her as fast as she could walk without running "you surprised me, caught me off-guard and I panicked."

"I...I thought..." Tara began as she turned to look at her, her eyes still red from her tears.

Sierra held Tara's face between her hands.

"Hush now; yes...my answer is yes – my parents will be...displeased, but, yes, my beautiful messenger, I will marry you!" with that she planted a huge kiss upon her lips that lasted an eon or two, or so it felt.

'Oh thank the divines!' Tara thought to herself as she wrapped her arms around Sierra's waist and back.

Suddenly they were interrupted by the sound of the ferry's bell that signalled their arrival loudly chiming as they drew up against the port's docks.

"How long were we kissing?"

"Not long enough" Tara sighed, smiling, her cheeks still wet from her tears "Well, least we can catch up on that later; come on lover, I have letters to deliver."

***

Bahvain Middlands

Ji'Roh hailed the trader's carriage as he stood to the side of the dirt road, his clothes stained and ragged now. Much to his relief, the carriage stopped just ahead of him.

"What can we do you for, stranger?" one of the traders asked as he walked up beside them.

"Could you kindly tell me how far I am from this 'Bahvil'; I saw the sign for it a whiles back."

"You've got quite the walk ahead of you" he laughed "Have you no horse?"

Ji'Roh gestured to the state of himself.

"I have had quite the bad luck on my journey, as you can see" he said in good humour.

The trader whispered to his companions a moment, then turned back to Ji'Roh.

"Have you any coin stranger? Perhaps we could allow you to join us if so – a precaution, I'm sure you understand."

"I have a little with me, but I must keep enough to bargain for a horse."

"A horse is not 'a little' coin, sir."

"My apologies, I mean there is little I can spare."

"And why do you need this horse, if I may ask?" the trader asked with a questioning brow.

"I am headed to Hamurfel, thus I need to replace my lost horse if I am to make it on time."

The traders whispered together again.

"Okay stranger, have you ten silver pieces, or five gold coin spare?"

"That I could manage."

The carriage door opened.

"Then come aboard my good sir, and tell us of your misfortune."

Ji'Roh sighed in relief as he clambered into the carriage; the rest would do him good, and he was getting closer to his return home.

***

Kromahr Docks, Orcain

The pair walked up the docks towards a grand pier, which had a theatre at the end of it, which stood next to the great stone walkway that twisted and turned up the cliff-face to Kromahr, the large and sprawling sea town that made up one of

Orcain's main seaports – the third biggest in all of the Orc Isles – which would be their last stop before their arrival in Ebo.

Tara wondered at how practical the theatre was, given the volatile nature of the ocean, but her thoughts quickly turned to the engineering wonder of Kromahr, and of its visual magnificence. The Orcs had, over many years in the first half of the Second Era, carved into the cliff face, with strong yet graceful masonry, building structures that were equal part ornate and functional; especially the colossal sea defences that kept the lashing waves from tearing down what they had built. As she gazed up at it all, she could see the lights of torches and candles being lit in anticipation of the soon-to-set sun, which was now nearing the horizon, and marvelled at the human hive ingrained within the rock, before returning her gaze to the pier before her, where dock workers treated the wood with a tar-like paint to protect it from the elements. The whole place bustled with life, even at this late hour, all manner of people and goods – both strange and familiar – being loaded and unloaded from ships and pulled towards their destinations by ox-drawn carts, guardsmen on horseback a rare but ever-present fixture.

"So what'dya think?" Sierra smiled as she led the horses by their reins "Real something else isn't it?"

"It's...beautiful."

"Isn't it just?" she looked up at the cliff face "We should be able to get a room for the night at the clifftop; there's an Inn there that always has room for soldiers, see?"-she pointed to a far corner of the town, at a cylinder shaped building emanating from the top of the cliff-"They'll have space for us I'm sure."

"Wait...overnight? But I thought-"

"I know, but – wait, don't you know?" they both stopped walking, Sierra raising a questioning eyebrow.

"Know what?"

"They caught what they thought was a Hamurfelion spy – turns out it was just a smuggler – and decided it would be best that all travellers who travel beyond Kromahr need to be 'checked in', as they say."

"No, I hadn't heard" Tara said as innocently and naïvely as she could "I guess word hadn't reached the front before I left."

Sierra looked at her a moment longer, as if weighing up what she said.

"Yeah, news can travel pretty slow when it comes to the front lines, cant it?" she shrugged as they started walking again.

"Sierra?"

"Hmm?"

"I never asked, did you grow up on the Isles or?"

"Haha, no, no I didn't" she smiled, chuckling a little at old memories "Don't misunderstand, I was born on the western isle of Iciro, on the coastal city of Yvern Rock; we moved off the isles when I was still quite young, and it wasn't until I was eighteen that I returned, right here in Kromahr."

"I guess the isles called you back" she looked at Sierra "Why'd your family leave the isles in the first place?"

"Da was a warrior, a soldier all the way through, and so when he had the option to be positioned guarding the frontier homes on the 'mainland' he jumped at it, and we went with him."

Tara nodded silently, looking up at the cliffs, and the town – or rather city, as she considered it – embedded in the rock, filled with homes and businesses.

"How ever did they build this? Were there always so many people here, is that how they did it?" she let out a little sigh "I've seen great cathedrals and castles, mausoleums and tombs, but this? I still cannot believe that such a thing exists."

"Yeah, it's always been a central hub – we'll want to hug the left-hand side as we go up here – even when they were building it those hundreds of years ago; though it has only gotten bigger over time; the war has exacerbated it though I must say, each time I come through it seems more and more cramped. As for the – hey! Watch it!" Sierra shouted at a sailor that had drunkenly walked into her.

"S-so s-s-sorry missh" he slurred as he gave a stumbling bow before then staggered off on his way.

"Ugh!"-Sierra rolled her eyes-"It sure has brought the drunks in too."

As they walked up the curving carved walkway Tara ran her fingers along the weather-smoothed stone, pondering the history behind each piece of sculpting, each shaped stone bent to the will of its mason, and all the struggles and joy it has seen over its long and enduring life.

"So, why did you come back?"

"I'd been apprenticing as a blacksmith, and an opportunity came along to join the military armourers here in Kromahr; da was rather proud when I told him I was joining. Obviously I moved over to fieldwork a few years later; my decision, never was good at staying in one place too long, so it suited me better to be in a line of work that facilitated that."

"Your family must be proud" Tara smiled as she kept one hand upon her pouch of messages, self-conscious of the prospect of them being blown away or lifted by a pickpocket in such a crowded place.

"They are." She sighed "Not that we see each other these days; even when I get leave, it is never long enough to travel back to see them. Talking through letters is not the same as talking in person, you know?"

"I understand, and I'm sorry to hear that" Tara held her free hand gently.

"...Thanks" she smiled back as she pulled her hand away to grab her waterskin from her waist-belt. As she took a swig she looked at Tara, thinking quietly.

She returned the waterskin to her belt, and her arm around Tara's.

"When the war is over" she said as they turned a corner, pulling the horses close to allow a two ox cart to pass "I'm not sure how we'll live, or where."

"The whole staying in one place – 'settling down' as it were – once we're married?"

"Yeah, that" Sierra nodded almost sheepishly.

"How about this: we try staying in one place, and if that doesn't work we travel, be as nomads, how's that sound?"

"I could do that, so long as we're together"-she gave Tara a slight squeeze-"But for now"-she pointed to a rather ornate looking building with statues carved into its walls-"we need to talk to the officials in there to be checked in for travel."

"Which entails...?"

"Paperwork mostly; your name, why you are here and the like. For you they'll need to know whose orders you are acting on, who the messages are for and if there is any for military leadership, things like that."

"Okay, seems straightforward enough" Tara replied calmly as an internal panic raged within; this was very much not part of the plan.

"They'll need to take a look through the letters, by the way" Sierra added as she remembered that detail.

"Oh..." Tara replied quietly as she cursed loudly inside her head, knowing that if the King's seal was discovered within that special message things would end unpleasantly for her "They wouldn't open any of them would they?"

"Not sure" Sierra gave her that raised eyebrow look "That special delivery you can't tell me about?"

"Yeah" Tara nodded "I'm sure it'll be my head if they open it."

Sierra chewed at the side of her mouth in thought.

"I'll see if I can get them to overlook that one, but I can't make any promises."

CHAPTER TEWNTY-TWO

Sentinel's Watch Inn Kromahr, Orcain

The inn was bright with candlelight, and adorned in ornately carved wooden beams, a lone lute player strumming a wordless song that fed into the calming atmosphere. As Sierra talked to the barmaid about getting a room and breakfast for the two of them, Tara wandered around the seating area, looking out of the windows, which had been reinforced against the strong winds that came off the sea, gazing out at the waves and ships going to and fro from the other isles and the mainland as dusk began to obscure all bar that which was lit by moonbeams and torchlight; it was almost magical, as if painted upon the glass and brought to life by the flickering flames of the candelabras.

"Beautiful, isn't it?" Sierra smiled as she walked up behind her.

Tara smiled back silently, before taking a seat at the table beside the window, Sierra siting opposite her.

"I asked if they were still doing food; seems like we'll be getting some kind of chicken soup." She said as she reached for Tara's hand "The horses settled into the stable alright, by the way."

Tara stayed quiet.

"You okay?"

"...yeah, just...tired" she smiled, thoughts plaguing her.

"You still worked up over that clerk shouting at you-?"

"Please, don't remind me" she interrupted, raising her hand slightly to signal she didn't want to go over it.

"I'm sorry I wasn't there straight away; they didn't open the message did they?"

"No...no, thankfully you intervened just as they were about to tear it open"-a small shudder ran down her spine as she thought on how close she had come to being discovered-"I nearly...they put the fright in me, they really did; and I'm used to being on a battlefield, dodging arrows to deliver pieces of parchment" she leant her head in her hand as she let out a nervous laugh "You must think I'm ridiculous."

"No, I don't; those officials and their clerks are rather imposing, even to the most battle-hardened warrior, so don't feel embarrassed about it."

Tara looked into her mismatched eyes, their green and blue shimmering brilliantly in the ambient light of the inn; they had made her careless, distracted her enough to make her misstep and risk discovery, and yet...

"I'm so glad..." she began, before noticing the barmaid bringing over two steaming bowls of soup.

"Here y'are ladies" she chimed in a thick Orcish accent as she placed the bowls down before them, before then unhooking a breadbasket from her arm and placing it between them "Be careful now, it's piping hot. Just give me a shout if ya need anythin' else" she beamed before going back to tending the bar-come-reception desk.

"You were saying?" Sierra asked as she skimmed the top of her soup and gave it a little blow to cool down.

"Nothing that can't wait."-she broke a piece of bread into quarters-"this sure does smell good."

"Aye" Sierra replied as she took a few delicate sips from her spoon "Mmm, that hits the spot."-She looked up at Tara, seeing her dribble some soup down her chin as she ate some heavily dunked bread, and gave a little chuckle-"What are you like girl?" she laughed as she leant over and wiped it off with a small napkin.

"Thanks..."-she gazed into Sierra's eyes once more-"tonight...lets have some fun, I mean, *real* fun."

Sierra stopped mid spoon lift.

"Didn't you say you were tired?"

"I am, but..."she dabbed another chunk of bread into her soup "I just...I feel like I'd be letting you down if I didn't, if we didn't...you know."

"Tara, so long as I get to hold you close and cuddle you at night, it doesn't matter how much 'fun' we get to have" she smiled, before then continuing to eat, Tara smiling back.

"I love you" she said as she bit into her soggy, chicken laden bread.

Sierra looked up from her soup as she chewed a piece of chicken.

"...Love you too."

The pair of them lay spooning one another, each comforted by the warmth of the other's touch. Their room for the night was small yet comfortable in size, filled with various furnishings of carved wood and stone; their clothes, for the most part, lay neatly upon a writing desk, Tara's satchel of letters in arms-reach upon the bedside cabinet. The bed itself was lined with some kind of fur, which gave a comforting, homely feel against ones skin, and was covered in a duvet of soft cotton and a woollen blanket beneath a deerskin.

Sierra's hand was wrapped around Tara, over her side and holding her hand next to her chest, and as they lay there Tara could feel her breath; it was a nice thing to feel, soothing so she thought. She contemplated the events at the check-in centre, and how it had been going smoothly until they came to the King's message. Sierra had been talking to another official, going over her orders and how things were near the front, as Tara stood before a large stone table as the official – and her assistant – dealing with her pestered her with questions. They had continued to insist that she spread out the letters before them so they might check them for contraband, as she tried to stall them for as long as possible; whilst the letters were mundane for the most part, it was still risky to let them look them over seeing as they were forgeries. Finally she relented, on the condition none would be opened, holding back the Kings message as she did.

"Was that so hard?" the assistant had sneered, Tara thinking on how badly he made her skin crawl.

They were about to give her her papers – ones to show any patrol or guard that stopped her outside of Kromahr – when the assistant spotted the hidden letter.

"What is that?" he had asked.

"I have orders to not reveal that" she had replied as confidently as possible, if not wholly convincingly.

"You must allow us to check it over" the official said disinterestedly as she looked at the long line of travellers waiting beyond them.

"But, my orders-"

"Whose orders?" the assistant snapped

"I'm under order not to say."

"How convenient" he replied, gesturing for a guard to snatch it from her; she tried to grab it back, but refrained herself at the last moment from doing something that would bring more attention to her.

The guard handed the assistant the letter, and he felt it for anything concealed within the folded parchment, until he found a lump; the King's seal, still hidden beneath its parchment covering.

"Well, what have we here?" he went to tear it open.

"Please, it'll be my head if that letter is opened by anyone other than its intended recipient!" she pleaded, no longer acting.

"Then tell us whose orders you are acting on."

She remembered how she felt the heat of panic, the beads of sweat forming on her brow as she stumbled for something to say, the look on the assistants face, one of pleasure at the thought of catching someone. But, thankfully for her, it was at that moment Sierra hand walked over and calmed the situation in a way only a warrior could. Her words hand been calm but forceful, backed up by the honour and trust held in her uniform and armour. Tara could not remember what it was Sierra had said, just the tone of her speech, and the relief as they exited the building with their travel documents.

Tara looked at the faint glow of moonlight breaking through gaps in the curtains, absently rubbing the back of Sierra's hand with her thumb. She had been terrified of discovery, but now felt safe in Sierra's strong caressing arms, kept awake only by the haunting prospect of the inevitable moment where she would learn the truth, that she had lied to her – that she'd been lying to her since the moment they'd met. She hoped she would understand, that she had no choice, but did not have the confidence all would be fine. She felt a heavy breath upon her neck as Sierra stirred a little. Tara loved love, whether she would ever admit it or not, and found it to be a scary, precious thing. She thought on its rarity, and its many shapes. She loved her King – Hamurfel really – in a way, a loyal way, which was why she had agreed to this journey, this task. She had always been a highly trusted and capable messenger, and as such had been the

King's first choice. That trust was special to her – *trust* was special to her. And it was this that made her uneasy, for there was no way, at least in her mind, that she could keep the trust of both her King and Sierra at the same time, not whilst this war – 'damned war' as she put it – was still ongoing.

She gave a sigh as she re-closed her eyes and nuzzled her head further into her downy pillow, hoping the night would bring her a reassuring sleep.

CHAPTER TWENTY-THREE

Chancellor's Palace
Ebo, Orcain

Val'Ur lay with one arm gently over Roselia's side as they slept; well, as Roselia slept – Val'Ur was awake with runaway thoughts.

She listened to – and felt – Roselia's breathing and heartbeat, and it helped clam her. Roselia was of a smaller frame than her, not too dissimilar to Amira in that respect, and feeling her against her, beneath her arm, made Val'Ur feel like she was with Amira once more; it made her heart hurt less, and she was sure Roselia felt the same, in a way.

She nuzzled a little closer, feeling the brush of Roselia's hair against her face.

She was glad to have her for a friend, thankful that she served as her handmaid, and loved her dearly. It was rare that she would say so, rare that she would show any strong emotion at all, but in these private quarters, these private moments when it was just her and Roselia, she had become more open and raw; a side effect of being away from Amira for so long perhaps. Sometimes it would feel burdensome and jarring to her own sense of self, other times it was freeing, joyfully so in a way.

Roselia shifted a little in her sleep, Val'Ur smiling to herself at the thought of her dreaming.

They had met when Val'Ur was but ten years old, and Roselia was the hardworking daughter of one of the Chancellery's maids, and by good luck they had found kinship in one another – many years ago now, but only a fleeting memory away.

Moonlight seeped in through the woven curtains above her bed as the moon was left unobscured by the nightly clouds being drifted away by a silent heavenly breeze.

Val'Ur opened her eyes, too tired to sleep, too full of thoughts to think. Her eyes stared beyond the softness of Roselia's hair, off into places far in the distance, and those far away in time, and let out a heavy sigh.

On the morrow she would train with some of the best swordsmen still in Ebo – a chance to refresh, and test, her skills and particular fighting style – and there would be spectators.

Being watched wasn't what troubled her, nor the fighting itself, but the *why* of the peoples' interest – the war.

It had, with her father's 'encouragement', ignited a certain aggressiveness in her people, a thirst to see their leaders being more ruthless. She did not like it. But she was sure that, deep down, they would know the difference between being ruthless and being strong; it was just a matter of having them see it.

And she could see the spark of that hope, in how they had not changed, not bent to her father's urgings of them to steer those sons that loved men, those daughters who loved women, away from their true selves for the sake of making more future warriors; they stayed steadfast to love for love's sake.

Roselia shifted again, lightly stirred by the moonlight.

Val'Ur held her close, lightly rubbing her thumb against her arm.

It made her want to laugh, the reason she loved sharing her bed with Roselia – a reason that could be seen as unexpected. It was more than the company and companionship, more than the balm to her loneliness and heartache; she made her feel safe.

Val'Ur reclosed her eyes, nuzzling once more into Roselia's hair, and dreamt of her future life with Amira.

CHAPTER TWENTY-FOUR

Palace of the Dred King, Hamurfel, Akiro Region

Aka Nor'un cursed Xürr as he strode through the halls of the King's Palace, one of his loyal guardsman tailing behind him. He had no doubt Zara had had a hand in Xürr's disregard for his orders, not that he could prove it. News of their soldier's victory at Cairngor Ridge had reached them only that morning, and whilst the King was pleased to have driven the Orcs back a full league, Nor'un was infuriated; his carefully laid plan had been spoilt, for instead of suffering heavy losses as the Orcs gave their 'surprise' counter attack as they acted unwittingly upon his information, Xürr's troops had launched an attack with a rudimentary catapult loaded with flaming tar and burning coals, and in the confusion it sowed Zara's troops had mopped up the Orcs from the opposite side they were ordered to attack from. But, on the upside, he now had the Dred King – and the whole Akiro region – to himself.

"Nor'un" his guardsman asked as they entered the War Room "What is our plan now that General Xürr has disobeyed command?"

Nor'un looked at the map of Cairngor, the newly liberated lands and troop positions relabelled accordingly.

"We still have the capital secured" he muttered to himself.

"Sir, with all due respect, if we were to strike after such a victory, the people would surely riot; we could not take the Palace without having to worry about a rebellion ourselves."

"Not to mention the Orcish Lords will not be trusting of me after this." He bowed his head down in thought as he leant over the map table "At least I have no need to concern myself with them inevitably betraying me now" he sighed.

His guardsman watched him silently a moment.

"Sir, have we any need to worry about General Zara or Xürr if they are kept at the front? Surely they will slip up at some point?"

Nor'un shook his head.

"No, they won't. And it will not take them long to find an excuse to bring at least some portion of their troops home." He glanced over the map, absently tracing the paths of the troops "I risked much to inform the Orcs of their positions, now that they are at least somewhat aware of my plans, I cannot risk it again."

"Sir, I-"

The guardsman was cut off as another of Nor'un's guardsmen came bursting into the room.

"General Nor'un, sir!" the man called as he hastily walked over as the door swung shut behind him "I have heard news from the Orcish lands!"

Nor'un raised an eyebrow.

"A trader from Blackwood has been causing a stir in the market, telling a tale – a rumour – that a whole village of Orcs were slain by our troops!"

"What?" Nor'un turned to him fully, throwing a quick glance at his other guardsman "Has the King been informed?"

"Yes, I overheard one of the servants telling him as made my way to you."

"Sir, would General Xürr do such a thing?" the guardsman asked as the one who brought the message stood to the side.

"No, no he wouldn't" he rubbed his stubbled beard lightly "And that seems too ruthless even for Zara...ha...haha" he laughed cruelly.

The two guardsmen exchanged a quick glance with one another.

"Sir?"

"Don't you see? The Orcs have set us up, staged a massacre – slain their own people – to foster hatred for us amongst their people! What cunning creatures those Lords are!"

"But, sir...why is that so amusing?"

"Because we no longer have to wait" he gave a dark smile "The King has ordered the slaughter of innocents – women and children – and we must act to stop further atrocities, do we not?"

The guardsmen nodded in understanding.

"Good. Now ready the men, we take the capital in two days; we have only one chance at this, so make sure those that would stand in our way can't."

"Yes sir" the two guardsmen saluted, as Nor'un looked back at the map, planning his next move.

CHAPTER TWENTY-FIVE

Bahvil Town, Bahvain region

News of the massacre had spread fast through the trading routes, faster than Ji'Roh could walk or run. As he bargained for a horse he overheard merchants tell the tale of Vilwood, the Orcish village gutted of its people, and how it had been the Hamurfelion's who had done it. Some refused to believe such a thing, others believing all too readily.

As he readied his saddle and provisions he wondered whether or not to inform the governor of the town, a Countess Asiy Balford, as to the true nature of the horrific event before he left for

Hamurfel. Would dragging this fledgling place of trade and commerce into the conflict do any measure of good? He reflected on this question a good hour or so as he made some final preparations and had a meal at one of the taverns, having decided it best to eat before he began his journey once more.

As he paid his bill and left to get upon his horse, he resolved to inform the Countess of what he had witnessed, and to advise her from intervening as such, but rather to have the truth of it spread; he knew, or at least hoped, that the merchants would be able to spread such news back to the Orc Isles faster than he could.

CHAPTER TWENTY-SIX

Seagoth Hills, Outskirts of Ebo, Orcain, Orc Isles

Tara was amazed at how large Ebo really was, a city built into a mountain from the base up, not unlike Kromahr in many respects, only more imposing and regal. They had had no troubles on the road from Kromahr, only being stopped once by a patrol to check their papers, and had made good time on their journey, much to Tara's relief and trepidation.

"So where's our first delivery, love?" Sierra asked as they gently rode their horses through the farming outskirts of Ebo.

"I think my 'special' delivery should take priority" she replied as she looked upon the mountain's peak and the Chancellor's Palace, home to the Council of Orcish Lords, that adorned it "How do we get up there?"

Sierra followed her gaze.

"Ah, that's how important that message is" she said mostly to herself "We can take the main road into the mountain, and leave our horses at the military stables therein. From there we can either climb the cavern steps or take the surface path."

"Cavern steps?"

"What the locals call the hallways and passages carved inside the mountain; don't worry, they're not all small and claustrophobic in size" Sierra smirked humorously.

"How many generations did it take to build a literal mountain's worth of city?" Tara asked, still incredulous at the scale of Ebo.

"Not sure personally; though I know it was built in the centre of the First Era. I'm sure the Archive of Orcain will have the records, should you want to visit after you've finish your business here."

"I'd like that" Tara smiled, her thoughts turning to her mission once more "But...what if my work doesn't finish with the delivery?"

"What do you mean?"

"I could get further orders for one thing."

"Then I shall stand by your side as you do those too."

"You are sweet." Tara sighed "But I would be lying if I said I wasn't apprehensive as to how my delivery will go down, and what will follow it."

Sierra was quiet for a moment, deep in thought as they began to transition from the outskirts to the city proper.

"So which Lord are we to deliver the message to?" she asked finally, just as they passed an outdoor market filled with all manner of goods and foods.

"The Chancellor" Tara replied after a moment's hesitation.

Sierra looked at her in shock.

"The Chancellor himself? Whatever is in that letter?"

"A message."

"Funny. But really, what is it all about?"

"Sierra, can you just wait until we're in the Chancellor's Palace? It...it's unsafe to talk about these things out in the open."

Sierra looked at her a moment longer, before giving a light shrug and returning her gaze to the path before them.

"It'll be a good hour before we get there, assuming we don't get stuck behind a crowd" she said absently.

Tara nodded, looking at the architecture and fashion of the Orcish Capital. It was ancient in many respects, yet highly advanced in others – the masonry and engineering of each building, road and path an intricate design built to outlast the people who made and inhabited it – whilst the clothes were mostly deep matt colours, lots of browns and marbled grey, speckled with deep reds and greens. There were grand sculptures, statues of fallen heroes and mythical beasts, and deities of old that formed focal points where the people would meet and gather; the city itself dominated by the obsidian stone that made up its fabric, yet held a pleasant feel about it as flowers and fruiting trees made up rows and ran alongside walkways that brought much needed light to the place. It was no

Hamurfel, no Akiro region – there was no gritty sand and the air was not dry and desiccating, no terracotta coloured buildings to speak of, and certainly no chance of sandstorms choking their crop fields – but it felt like home to Tara, not that she could place exactly why.

As they came up towards the cavernous entrance to the Mountain's interior, Tara could not help but feel the tingle of nervousness begin to swell within her once more; it would not be long before she would be forced to reveal the truth – one way or another. It made her sick, nauseated, the thought of losing Sierra or her heart, knowing she would be hurt once she learned that she'd been lying to her; but knew that there would be no turning back from where she now found herself.

"Now that's a foreboding entrance" she muttered as they got closer, the imposing doors of iron and stone rising taller than most buildings she had known.

"Aye; fret not though, they bring in daylight with an array of mirrors" Sierra chimed.

"This place just keeps getting wilder and wilder" Tara chuckled as she thought on the absurdity of the effort and design such a thing would take "Say, do we dismount before or after we enter?"

"Just before; just stick next to me and I'll lead you to the stables."-She paused a moment-"I know a place inside where we can talk in private."

"We should just keep going with the delivery; I shouldn't have to remind you how important it is."

"I know, but trust me, what I need to say is just as important, if not more."

"You have me worried now" Tara said, her eyes trying to read Sierra's face desperately.

"Just trust me Tara, that's all I ask."

"...Okay. Just don't go breaking my heart."

"I couldn't do that my love, not without breaking mine."

*

They had just left their horses with the military stables, and were now heading up a granite staircase towards a room where Sierra said they could talk in private.

"-so yeah, being a warrior allows me access to these places" she explained as she opened a stone door to let Tara through.

"So, it's like some kind of breakroom?" Tara asked as she took a seat next to the room's lone wooden table.

"Aye, something like that" she replied as she closed the door behind them, pulling the latch shut so that they wouldn't be disturbed, before taking a seat opposite Tara "Now, we need to talk."

"Okay" Tara replied, nervously looking into her eyes.

"I know."

"...Know what?" Tara asked innocently.

"You might have been able to pretend to everyone else you've met, but me? You're too vulnerable with me to properly hide it; I can see through your lies."

"Sierra-"

"Tara, do not insult my intelligence by denying it" Sierra interrupted "I can see you love me – it's why I can tell, why I can see through you and your words – but that doesn't make it hurt less."-Tara regarded her silently, weighing up her options as she listened-"So, yes, I know."

Tara bit her lip, putting her face in her hands as she took a deep breath.

"What is it that you know?" she asked at last.

"I know you're not Orcish, not by any measure, and that you are delivering a message from Hamurfel"-she put a hand out to Tara-"Tell me what I don't know, tell me the *why* of your journey. Tell me whether you were ever going to tell me any of this."

Tara looked at Sierra's outstretched hand a moment, before tentatively taking it in hers, and took a second to clear her throat.

"I was going to tell you, once my mission was complete." She began, choosing in that moment, her heartbeat quickening, to trust in her above all others, and keep nothing from her ever again "I am the King's messenger, and the message I carry is for Val'Ur – fiancé to the True Queen."

"But you said it was for the Chancellor?"

"I have a different *message* for him."

"I see." Sierra gave a little sigh "I cannot let you do that, you understand." She gave a light squeeze of Tara's hand.

"Even if it would end the war?"

"Even then."

"What of my message to Val'Ur?"

"I can see that it is delivered."

"I must be the one to do so Sierra, I gave my oath to the Dred King himself."

“How can I let you? You will assassinate the Chancellor if you are out of my sight for but a moment, and what of the other Lords?”

Tara said nothing, though the expression in her eyes spoke volumes..

“Tara, I love you, and I will do not want to lose you, but that will happen if you harm any of them – I cannot stop them if they catch you.”

“Then I won’t get caught.”

“Tara...”

“Are you going to hand me in?”

“What?”

“Am I your prisoner?”

“No, by the divines no!” Sierra clasped her other hand around Tara’s, holding her tightly “No, I just...I couldn’t, they’d kill you. Worse even.”

“So, where does that leave us? Why didn’t you say any of this earlier?”

“I had to see your reaction to getting so close; I hadn’t been sure up ‘till now” she leaned over the table “But as for where *we* go from here? I don’t know. All I beg of you is to not do something that would jeopardise *us*.”

Tara looked down at their entwined hands, thinking upon her loyalties. ‘What was the right thing to do?’ was the question she found herself asking, her past experiences being all but useless to her now. She looked back up at Sierra, gazing deep into her mismatched green and blue eyes.

"How about this; I deliver the letter to Val'Ur with you by my side, then we elope from this war, move to Blackwood or Norain, try settling down...does that sound like a plan to you?"

"How do I know this isn't a lie?"

"Didn't you say you could see through my lies?"

"The problem is that you lied in the first place. I accept in the beginning you had no choice, but after the time we've been *together* – how intimate we've been – it makes it difficult to trust you as much as I want to."

"That...that's fair. I get it, I really do, and I'm sorry; I'm so, so sorry. I love you and I'm scared of losing you, but I had my loyalties and love for Hamurfel...I just...being found out is scary, right? But you...you terrify me, petrify me. Normally I can weave my way through most any situation, any danger without a second thought, but you? I am so scare of being hurt by you, or of hurting you – losing you and your love – that I am left feeling weak and fragile, confused and lost as to what I am meant to do." Tara's voice was choked with emotion, her eyes welling up as her words trailed off.

Sierra got up from her seat and walked round to Tara, and lifted her onto the table, moving in close as she put her arms around her.

"Tara...you need not fear feeling weak, and you certainly aren't fragile. I love you, you hear me? I. Love. You."-She ran her right hand through Tara's hair-"You promise me we leave it at delivering that letter, and I'll follow you anywhere."

"I promise. With all my heart Sierra, I swear this to you, on my oath."

They looked deep into each other's eyes, each seeming to glisten in the ambient light, small tears forming for the both of them.

"Then I am yours"-she leaned in and gave an impassioned kiss-"You shall be my wife and I shall love you from now and until and beyond the end. Never fear telling me anything, never hold back the truth, and if you feel weak, know that you are not. If you feel as if you have lost all sense of direction I shall be your guide. If you need support I shall be your stave, if you need love I shall be your heart."

"I...I didn't know you could be so...romantic" Tara cried with relief and love, feeling her soul fill with warmth; a warmth she had thought long lost.

"I just needed to know you really did love me, that you weren't using me to get here."

"I'd never-"

"I know, I know. Now kiss me, my Hamurfelion beauty" she said as she pulled Tara closer, the two of them embracing for a good, long time.

With their two hearts now beating as one, and their futures inseparably entwined, they loved one another, forgetting for a moment that they had other business to attend to.

CHAPTER TWENTY-SEVEN

South Cairngor Disputed lands

Rahool surveyed the battlefield from atop his trusty steed, Xürr coming up alongside him as he calculated their enemy's next move.

"Zara's troops have broken the western line; won't be long until we push them out of Cairngor entirely." Xürr said, pulling gently on his horse's reins to bring it to a stop next to Rahool.

"Seems almost too easy" he muttered.

"Almost" Xürr sighed "Shame they burnt our catapult to cinders; could have used that when we get to their fort near the tin mines."

"Quite."-he turned to Xürr-"Any word on Nor'un?"

"None. Which is worrying in of itself I must say."

"What does Zara think?"

"She thinks we need to head back to Akiro, but we don't have much of a choice, seeing as half our men are injured or maimed and the Orcs have no interest in putting this war on hold."

"Don't talk so carelessly; those men and women have given their lives and limbs to Hamurfel, as have the Orcs given theirs for their homeland, treat them with the honour and respect they deserve."

"My apologies Rahool; war has something of a desensitising effect on me." Xürr looked back to the battlefield, which was quiet bar the odd skirmish – this western side of the fight having long since been pushed further south – the dead still waiting for rescue, and pondered how similar the capital would look if those few guardsmen loyal to the King tried to fight back against Nor'un "What do we do Rahool? We bought some time disobeying Nor'un's orders, but does it even matter? We can't leave the front because of the Orcs, and can't stay because of Nor'un."

Rahool stayed quiet, silently thinking as he watched a few arrows fly through the air in the distance.

"We need the Orcs to agree to a temporary hold to the fight."

"Like they'd agree to that" Xürr scoffed.

"We can but try."

"Rahool old friend, I love your optimism, but you are wrong."

"We shall see."

"Rahool...some of the men have been telling tales of the Orcs calling us 'butchers' and slaughterers of..." Xürr trailed off a moment "Haven't you notice a change in the way they fight us?"

"No, not that I can say; been too busy pushing them back to listen to 'em. Why, what's on your mind?"

"I don't know, not yet; going to capture a 'warrior' or two, see what they have to say."

"Keep Zara in the know; she is wise and her experience valuable."

"I know Rahool, I know – she never lets me forget it."

***

Palace of the Dred King, Akiro Region, Hamurfel

"You...How could you do this Nor'un!" the King accused, disbelieving at his current situation.

"Easily." Nor'un smirked as he closed the cell door on him "Fret not, your sister's care will continue."

"If you so much as-"

"You are in no position to make threats *king*; your time is over. Finished. Your loyalists are all dying on the front lines, the whole of Akiro bends its knee to *me* now, and soon so will the rest of Hamurfel."

"Cowardly betrayer!" the King spat "When the people come for you I shall show you no mercy!"

Aka Nor'un laughed.

"You just don't get it do you? This, all of what I have done, has been for the people." He turned to leave, signalling his guardsmen to follow.

"They'll see through you Aka, they'll know this is just a grab for power!" the King called, his rage slowly waning.

"No old friend, they won't" Nor'un said as he left, his guardsmen closing the door behind them, leaving the Dred King in the drab dark of the prison cells, alone.

***

Outskirts of Akiro

Ji'Roh had rode into Akiro, and had found the atmosphere uncharacteristically tense. As he made his way to the capital and the King's Palace, he could not help but notice the people act apprehensively around their guardsmen, and even more so in the company of strangers. It had him concerned in more ways than one, not least for his own safety.

"Excuse me" he asked a passer-by as he made his way through the market, his horse now stabled; they just kept on walking.

He stared after them for a moment, then looked back towards the King's Palace.

The Blackwood clothing Kaymar had given him had helped him evade much suspicion – even in its tattered state – but as he walked through the Hamurfelion capital he felt as if everyone's eyes were searing him; or at least that was how it had felt at first, but now, as he drew closer to the palace? Now everyone seemed desperate to keep from making eye contact with one another. If he hadn't been so desperate to deliver Val'Ur's message and return home to his beloved Roselia, he would have been unnerved by it, perhaps even taken the time to work out why. Instead he thought himself lucky, as it made it far less likely he'd be stopped.

CHAPTER TWENTY-EIGHT

The Obsidian Corridors, Cavern steps, Ebo

Tara unwrapped herself from Sierra, wiping away tears of relief as she did so. Words could not describe how happy and joyous she was in this moment, in the lifting of her secret burden, and at the chance of a future with Sierra by her side. But, as the ever cynical part of her mind told her, she still had to deliver the King's message to Val'Ur and then – depending upon her reaction – flee the Orcish lands or persuade Sierra to follow her back to Hamurfel with Val'Ur's response; in other words, there was still plenty of opportunity for things to go wrong, terribly wrong.

They walked down obsidian corridors etched with depictions of Orcish history, up staircases moulded from the mountain's insides, passing all manner of facilities and rooms – Sierra had told her most of these were for Ebo's guardsmen, servants for the Orcish Lords, and the stonemasons that maintained the city – until they at last came back outside, now two thirds the way up the mountain city, and looking out at the cityscape below.

"This...I still can't get over the scale of Ebo, it's incredible" Tara said, absently distracted by the vast vista as they walked a westward path going further up and towards the Chancellor's Palace.

"Yeah, I don't think there's any place like it" Sierra replied as she led Tara by the hand "I've heard rumours of places in Norain that match in scale, but I doubt there's anything to match this." She looked back at Tara "So, the message..."

"What about it?"

"Do you know what's in it?"

"No."

"Think it's anything that could stop a war?"

"I'm not sure anything can stop this war."

"Don't be so pessimistic" she scoffed as they climbed a few steps.

Tara felt that nervous knot returning to her, her stomach feeling as if it were churning.

"Sierra, I'm scared."

"Scared...? Why?"

"The last time I loved someone I lost them, and all I can think of is how everything could go wrong. I mean, what if I can't get the message to Val'Ur? What if she's not the friend my King-"

"Not so loud!" Sierra hushed her, nervously glancing around to see if anyone heard her "You forget that no-one here calls anyone their 'King'."

"Right...but see? Normally I would be stealthily blending in, but with you...I lose track of my senses."

"So it's my fault then?"

"That's not what I mean. You just preoccupy my mind, because I'm selfish – really, really selfish – because I...I'd rather have you, be with you, than deliver this letter."

"Then why deliver it?"

"Because I gave my word Sierra; I can't break my word for anyone or anything."

"I can respect that" Sierra nodded quietly.

The pair continued up a gentle incline, the paved rock smoothed from millennia of use, passing grand buildings of carved mountain and glass – most being stained glass – that looked as if they had grown there as the mountain itself had formed. The ornateness of the carvings and pillars that made them intrigued Tara, made her question what had motivated the Orcs of old to partake in such an effort. The stonework was hard and ordered, yet had a softness in the intricate details and delicate, discreet curves that made the outer edges of each structure, which left each one both imposing and inviting with their curiosity. Along the path were planters, their green foliage a distinct contrast to the obsidian stone around them, which brought much needed vibrancy to Ebo, especially up upon the mountain. Inside them, nestled among the thick greenery were small alpine flowers, the odd heather taking up a planter of its own in a vibrant purplish red and occasional burgundy, and the odd birds nest, its occupants use to the presence of people who would do them no harm.

Tara found the place almost magical, as if such a place was not possible without some harmonious spell to bring it all together.

As they neared the Chancellor's Palace the road became busier; guardsmen standing guard, a few patrolling, deliverymen and women bringing supplies up from the base of the mountain, servants going about their duties – it was all what one would expect, but still unsettling busy for one who by rights shouldn't be there.

"Just follow my lead, okay?" Sierra said as she released Tara's hand, the pair striding up to the main entrance and approached one of the guards standing either side of it. "Excuse me" she asked her "I am escorting this messenger, whom I must deliver to Val'Ur."

The guard looked at her warily for a moment, weighing up Tara and her attire.

"From whence does the message come warrior?" she asked Sierra.

"From the front lines; the message is of a delicate nature."

"This one"-the guard gestured at Tara-"she does not seem the sort, nor a true Orc."

"I am indeed half-Orc" Tara lied "On my mother's side."

The guard raised a questioning brow.

"I assure you, I may not be a warrior, but I make a nimble messenger" Tara's heart fluttered nervously as she spun what she hoped would be a convincing thread of lies.

The guard turned her attention back to Sierra.

"You're one of the Sojourn patrol, are you not?" she asked, gesturing at the symbol on her patrol armour.

"Aye, that I am."

"Yet you have escorted this messenger to the capital?"

"Aye, my commander – Commander Rathena – ordered me to ensure the messenger safe travel, and that Val'Ur would receive the message personally."

"And your name warrior?"

"Sierra. Sierra Blackwood."

The guard nodded her head slowly as she contemplated their story.

"Wait here." She said dryly, before ordering the other guard to keep an eye on them whilst she went inside the palace.

"Well?" Tara whispered to Sierra.

"Think she's going to check that Commander Rathena exists, and that I'm one of her warriors, then check with her superiors as to whether to permit us entry; it's what I'd do anyway." She replied in a hushed tone as she watched the other people in the courtyard-like space "Try not to be nervous – they may be all serious and imposing, but they're just doing their job; and with me by your side, they have no reason to doubt you."

Tara gave a little smile to that, staying silent for fear of letting something slip. As they stood there waiting, watching the servants, guards and officials come and go, the guard made her way to Val'Ur.

*

"A messenger?" Val'Ur asked the guard.

"Yes Lady Ur, they say she comes from the front with information of a delicate nature" the guard replied, still bowing before her.

Val'Ur stood there a moment, the lines of her face-paint moving in line with her frown of thought; it was far too soon to have received a reply from the mission she had sent Ji'Roh on, and the fact the messenger was not him helping prove it was not related, so she thought.

"Their story checks out? Commander Rathena, I trust she patrols Sojourn? And warrior Sierra is one of her number?"

"Yes m'lady."

"Bring them to me; I would like to hear what they have to say myself."

"As you wish."

*

Tara leant against one of the shiningly smooth obelisks that lined the exterior area outside the Palace's main entrance, quietly watching Sierra chat with the other Orcs. She could see how natural it was for her – be it because they were her kin or be it because of her nature – to talk with such a commanding yet gentle manner, to draw others into conversation whether they knew her or not, whether they had something to say or not. It made her smile, for she knew that it was at least in part because of this that she had felt able to be so open with her, that she had risked it all by baring much of her soul, and her mission, with Sierra; she made one feel safe, made her feel safe, and able to confide any and all things in her. Those that talked with Sierra even seemed to brighten up slightly, even those whom had the face of misery seemed to gain some measure of cheer as she recounted tales and jokes, and enquired as to the goings on of the city and of the Orcish Lords.

It was just then that the guard came back, looking around for them a brief moment before then beckoning the pair of them over, Sierra politely excusing herself from a conversation with a servant.

"Lady Val'Ur has granted you an audience; follow me" the guard said, turning on the spot and walking back into the palace, the two lovers following close behind.

*

Roselia sat patiently at her desk, quill in hand, blank parchment before her, ready to record anything at a moment's notice, Val'Ur standing behind her as she waited for the messenger and her escort.

"What do you suppose it is Val?" she asked as she twirled the quill, looking at her ink pot, its lid still tightly shut.

"I don't think it's from Ji'Roh, Rose" she replied, absently checking the mighty blade sheathed to her belt.

"I didn't suggest that it was."

"But you were hoping it was, weren't you?"

"...that's beside the point."

Just as she was about respond there was a knock at the meeting room's door. After quickly readying her posture, Val'Ur called them to enter.

"Lady Ur, these are the messenger and escort I told you about." The guard announced as they entered the room, Sierra and Tara standing next to each other as the guard closed the door behind her as she left; though she waited outside the door, just in case.

"So, I hear that you have a message of a delicate nature for me?" Val'Ur asked as she weighed them up, detecting the chemistry between the two of them with ease.

"Yes m'Lady" Sierra said confidently "Tara here has travelled far and risked much to get this to you" she gestured for Tara to hand Val'Ur the letter.

Tara took a few steps forward, finally relinquishing the King's letter from her care as she held it outstretched to Val'Ur. Val'Ur walked over, taking hold of the letter and unfolding it, breaking the plain seal upon its outer covering and revealing the seal of the Hamurfelion King beneath. With that she recoiled a little in shock as she realised he had sent this letter – and messenger – to her, quickly shooting a glance at Tara before reading the message. The room fell into a tense silence, Tara nervously waiting to hear what would become of her, Sierra doing likewise as Roselia realised the vibes Val'Ur was giving off.

Finally Val'Ur lowered the letter, feeling the need to take a seat as she did so, before then looking back at Sierra and Tara.

"You're Hamurfelions? The two of you?" she asked.

"Only I" Tara responded quickly, Sierra giving her a worried look as she did so "Sierra here knew nothing."

"Is that so?" Val'Ur mused upon the letter's contents, and the issue of having a member of what was for near all intents and purposes the enemy in her meeting room. She got up, walking over to Roselia, placing the letter before her "Make a copy of this" she asked, Roselia obliging her readily, before then turning back to Sierra and Tara "Now, what do I do with you two?"

"M'Lady, if I may" Sierra began "I would ask you permit us to leave, to go somewhere outside of this conflict."-Tara shot her a glance, trying to tell her to stop-"I, we...I know it may seem strange, but this girl and I are engaged, and-"

"Sierra!" Tara grabbed her by the arm.

"It is okay Hamurfelion, you are safe here" Val'Ur said calmly.

The pair of them looked at her, somewhat disbelieving.

"Rose here will find you temporary lodgings" she gave a momentary glance at the King's letter "Your King, he has beseeched me to help put an end to the war, and so I will do what I can."

"Truly?" Tara asked.

"Yes." She took a deep breath "But I cannot do so alone, and as the King has trusted you, so shall I."-she returned to her seat-"A few months back I sent a message to your King and some of my allies to bring me aid, for I am but a prisoner without an obvious cage."

"What do you mean?"

"The Chancellor – my father – he has pledged my hand to another, to a man I do not love, in order to gain political favour and horde the power he covets. The people are too trusting of him for me to declare his corruption – and that of some of the other Lords – without any proof, or at least without enough loyalist to remove them from power."

"That is terrible Lady Ur" Sierra began "But...what can we do? We are but a patrolling warrior and a messenger."

"You were able to deceive your way to a meeting with me, able to avoid and penetrate all manner of defences with nothing but words, and as such you have shown great skill. This is what I have need of you to do: find evidence of my father's corruption – start with Lord Tallon, the gluttonous swine – and bring it to me so that he may be exposed and imprisoned for his crimes against our people. Only then will I be in a position to end this war without further bloodshed."

Sierra and Tara looked at one another nervously, before Tara asked a question.

"The King's letter, did it mention his orders regarding the other Lords?"

"Yes." Val looked at her sternly "And I'm overriding his orders; *you* shall not kill any of the Lords – it would only further their excuses for this blasted conflict."

"Understood" Tara nodded "Where should we begin?"

"Lord Tallon has a meeting with the other Lords tonight, along with my father. Rose will show you my father's chamber, as I show Sierra Lord Tallon's; be warned, discovery will most likely be fatal."

"Okay..."-Tara took hold of Sierra's hand-"In the name of peace, right Sierra?"

Sierra looked at her, her green and blue eyes shimmering with love and worry.

"Aye my love, for peace."

CHAPTER TWENTY-NINE

Palace of the Dred King, Akiro Region, Hamurfel

Ji'Roh walked up towards the main entrance to the King's Palace, nervously holding tight to the message canister fastened to his belt as the dust-laden wind blew hard against him. The palace stood tall, its grand, sunrise coloured marble exterior reflecting what sunlight dared to show itself through the dulled skies, and at the entrance stood four heavily armed guardsmen, adorned with faceguards, which only served to make Ji'Roh more nervous.

"Halt!" one of them called as he got within a few yards of them "State your business here."

Ji'Roh took a moment to clear his throat, raising a hand to guard his face from the wind.

"I carry an urgent message for the King" he shouted through a heavy gust.

The guards looked at each other a moment, before the one that had ordered him to stop spoke again.

"You have come from outside Akiro?"

"The message comes from beyond Hamurfel's borders" Ji'Roh replied "It has taken me many weeks to make it here, despite my haste."

"...Wait here messenger."

With that the guardsman went inside the Palace as the others stood watch, Ji'Roh sensing that they were hiding something from him.

*

The King sat slumped against a wall, his rage long since passed. Now he was all but defeated, worrying only for his people and his sister, her doctors permitted to inform him of her condition and the courses of treatment they prescribed so long as they were accompanied by an armed guard. He let out a heavy sigh, a lone tear rolling down his cheek, just as he heard the prison door's heavy lock turning. He looked up to see Samara – the more experienced physician of the two doctors – entering without a guard.

"Where's your guard?" he asked in an almost distant voice.

"I have a few minutes where they won't be looking for me; Kalib is distracting Nor'un with requests for medical supplies."

"Are...are you going to break me free?" his voice was scared of being hopeful.

"No...sorry, but to do so would be to sign your death warrant" she placed a hand on his cell's bars "But you should know, there is a messenger with a message for you."

"But...do they not know?"

"No, the messenger comes from outside Hamurfel, and Nor'un is going to act as if he is King."

"How do you know this?"

"It's amazing what one can overhear when you're a physician, especially a trusted one looking over a guard within earshot of Nor'un."

"So why tell me?" he almost laughed "I have no means of getting to the messenger."

"Actually you do, in a way. I could bring him here, let you hear the message."

"That's an awful risk Samara; if you're caught, what will happen to my sister? You and Kalib are all she has, if but one of you..." he drifted off as pessimism clouded his mind.

"I'll see what I can do; you have my word, if I cannot do so without endangering my care of your sister I will stay my hand."

*

Ji'Roh marched between the two guardsmen escorting him to the throne, one hand still nervously holding onto the message's container. He could feel something wrong in the air, but could not place what it was. He could see the King sat upon his throne, but something was off; he seemed different to the stories his dear Rose had told him whenever she returned with Val'Ur from a state visit, but nevertheless continued.

"You bring a message from beyond our borders for me?" the false king Nor'un asked.

"Yes, respected King of Hamurfel; I carry a message from Val'Ur, daughter of the Chancellor of the Orcish Lords" Ji'Roh spoke with a forced but respectful confidence, but as he finished his words he could see it in the king's eyes; something was wrong – very, very wrong.

"A message from Val'Ur...you, you're Orcish are you not?" Nor'un's eyes did not shift from his, and it was unnerving.

"I, err, yes; I am a trusted servant of Val'Ur. The message is of the upmost importance..." he looked around nervously "Is...is something amiss sire?"

"We are at war with your people. Do you not think that this is an unwise place for you to be?"

"But...Val'Ur and your sister-"

"Irrelevant" Nor'un interrupted, keeping up the act "But hand over that message, and we will not execute you for being a spy, understood?"

Ji'Roh frantically unfastened the message canister from his belt and began to open it, but just at that moment Samara let loose her distraction, having freed a handful of the King's loyalist and sent them into the throne room. Nor'un roared with disgust and his men followed his command to subdue them, as Kalib quickly grabbed Ji'Roh and pulled him into a corridor where Samara was lying in wait.

"Follow me messenger; the real King is this way" she said as she dragged him behind her, Kalib making his way back to Amira's room.

"What is going on?" Ji'Roh asked as they made their way through a maze of corridors.

"The General Nor'un staged a coup and has taken the palace and Akiro for himself, and seeks to subjugate all of Hamurfel too." She near kicked open the door to the prison when they got to it "Here's the messenger; we haven't much time before they realise he's missing."

Ji'Roh handed the message over to him through the bars, the King quickly unfurling it and reading as fast as his eyes could allow.

"That Bastard Chancellor!" he exclaimed "But how can I send aid when those loyal to Hamurfel are stuck in combat with the Orcs?" he rubbed his face in worry "You must take this to my Generals in Cairngor, tell them Nor'un has taken the city, that he has taken Akiro."

"But I am but a messenger, and an Orc; surely they would cut me down?" he asked, nervously rubbing his hands.

"Take this"-the King removed his signet ring, handing it to Ji'Roh through the bars-"They will trust you if you show them this."

Ji'Roh turned to Samara.

"Could I not take him with me?" he asked desperately.

"But Nor'un-"

"Just do it Samara, it's my life to risk" the King ordered; Samara just nodded solemnly, and proceeded to pick the lock.

*

Nor'un stood angrily over a beaten loyalist, holding him up by the collar.

"I won't ask again; how did you escape?" he fumed.

The loyalist spat at him defiantly; Nor'un throttled him in turn, before turning to one of his approaching guards.

"Sir, the Orc is missing, and the King's cell is empty."

Nor'un held back his frustration, closing his eyes in thought as he held his chin, trying to think what means of escape the King would take.

"Hmm" he laughed "I know where he'll be."

With that he gave a cruel smile, and strode off to find his once friend and King.

*

The two of them ran as fast and as stealthily as they could, Samara having headed back to Amira's room to ready her story with Kalib when Nor'un inevitably accused them. They had taken the old way out through the kitchens, having to scramble through a low window as the door had been long since sealed shut, and were now running down through the dried water channels that brought water from the flood plains during the spring and late summer.

"Are you sure this is the quickest way out?" Ji'Roh asked as they turned a corner.

"Yes; it's the only real chance we have to escape the city before Nor'un finds us."-They started to come up to a fork in the path-"Take the left side; we'll come up to a steel gate."

"How do we get through it?"

"There'll be a lever for it nearby."

As they came up to the gate they searched the walls for the lever until the King found it.

"Got it; now let's get out of here" with that Ji'Roh ducted under the small gap the lever had pulled open, the King following quickly after.

"Now if we take the eastern pass..." the King began as he straightened up as he came out the other side, before seeing what lay in wait for them "...no, No!" he exclaimed as he saw Nor'un riding up towards them on his horse, his men but a few yards behind him.

"What do we do?" Ji'Roh panicked "What in Oblivion do we do?"

"You run" the King grabbed him "Take my signet ring to Xürr and Zara in Cairngor, get them to aid Val'Ur, free us from this damned war, and free my people!"

"But-"

"Take the eastern route until you come to an obelisk marking the Royal Tombs, then head south; you're our only hope messenger, so run fast."

"They'll kill you, I-"

"Just keep running, no matter what happens, now GO!" the King shoved him off as he readied himself for Nor'un, Ji'Roh running with all the momentum his muscles could muster, every fibre of his being in a state of flight.

"Come on" the King whispered to himself "no fear, just retribution" his fists clenched as Nor'un drew close, two of his guardsmen riding after Ji'Roh "You want me Nor'un? Then take me like a man!" he shouted, his innate ferocity returning to him.

Nor'un's men surrounded him, with Nor'un himself dismounting and striding up to the King, laughing as he did so.

"I told you what would happen if you tried to escape", he said as he swung a fist at the King, who deflected it with an upward swing of his arm.

The King returned a blow, nocking Nor'un back as it connected with his lower jaw.

"You think yourself king, but you are nothing but a power hungry cowered"-he hit Nor'un again-"The people hate you"-he struck again, this time in the left side of Nor'un's head-"You were my friend" Nor'un blocked his follow up strike, pushing the King back.

"You dare? You have left your people to rot!" he swung at the King, catching him off-guard "All this has been for them!"

"Liar!" the King screamed as he lunged at Nor'un, landing blow after blow "You have always been selfish, this is no different." He lifted Nor'un off the ground, holding him up in the air by the throat "You broke my heart Nor'un...you were a brother to me" Nor'un struggled for air, his men refraining from aiding him due to the code of such a duel "You...the people will be freed from your clutches."

"N-n-no" Nor'un uttered as he finally managed to unsheathe his dagger and run it into the Kings arm, causing him to yell out in pain and drop him.

"See? Even now you cheat" the King spat as he readied what defence he could with one arm "You have no honour!"

"No" Nor'un thrust at him, holding back the King's good arm as he drove the dagger into him "But I win."

The King let out a gasp for air, his lungs filling with blood, Nor'un cradling him as he fell to his knees.

"I did not lie" Nor'un said as he looked into the King's eyes "I do this for the betterment of our people"-the King looked back at him, struggling to speak-"And I give you my word, in the name of our past brotherhood, that no harm shall come to your sister; I will see to it she gets the best treatment possible."

"Wh...Why?" the King asked through gargled and choking air.

"Because your decisions brought us nothing but war; I shall bring us peace."

The Kings eyes rolled back, his body going limp in Nor'un's arms. Nor'un would never show it, and none would ever know it, but this turn of events saddened him greatly; but he would do anything if he thought it would lead to the betterment of his people.

"Find the messenger" he said, still holding the King "See to it he does not make it far."

CHAPTER THIRTY

Chancellor's Palace
Ebo

Tara looked beneath the cast-iron bed, searching the small gap beneath it for any clues to the Chancellor's misdeeds, as Roselia stood guard at the door, watching for any possible intrusion or risk of discovery. The room was very ordered, as if it had not been lived in so much as made to look as if it had been lived in, like the set of a stage play; even the desk seemed unnaturally ordered despite its stacks of papers and pot of heavily used quills. Tara straightened up, still on her knees, and looked around the room, trying to think where she would hide incriminating evidence if she were Chancellor. Her eyes drifted across the desks and bureaus, wondering if they would have enough time before the Council of Lords finished their meeting, until she found herself staring at the ornately carved mahogany wardrobe, two mirrors hung either side of it that reflected the painting upon the opposite wall. She weighed it up a moment, before rising to her feet and striding on over to it; she opened it, sliding the neatly hung clothes and finery to one side as she looked for any hint of something concealed. She knelt down once more as she checked the base of the wardrobe's interior. She felt along the polished wood, its smooth surface uniform and uninterrupted, and let out a frustrated sigh; she had checked near half of the room, in all the most obvious places, and a few of the least obvious too.

"No luck?" Rose called quietly, having heard Tara's sigh.

"No" Tara replied bluntly "I would have sworn it would be in this wardrobe, it...it just seems like the right place."

Rose stepped away from her post at the door and up next to Tara, looking about the wardrobe for any clues.

"You checked the writing desk?" she asked as her eyes scanned the wood.

"Yes, and the dressing table, and drinks bureau" Tara sighed again as she leant her head into her hand in thought, eyes closed "The man's good at hiding things, that's for sure."

"What about behind the painting?"

"Too obvious, and the thing's too big to be convenient."

"But did you look?" Roselia insisted.

"No..." she looked back at the painting – one of a grand scenery, presumably of the mountain before the Orcs converted it into the city of Ebo, with a few small specks she presumed to be the early Orcish people – contemplating it a moment "Okay, help me lift the damned thing."

With that the two of them positioned themselves either side of the painting, each taking hold of one of its corners, lifting it and its heavy frame off the wall.

"You okay holding that?" Tara asked, slightly concerned for Rose in her now obviously pregnant condition.

"Aye; I may be carrying a little one, but I'm still capable" she replied as they rested the painting on the dressing table "huh, how about that" she laughed slightly as she looked at the now bare wall.

"Well damn; I guess too obvious is the best hiding spot sometimes" Tara concurred as they looked at the now exposed wall safe "Damned thing isn't even locked" she mused as she opened it, revealing an assortment of papers and coin-purses "You look through that stack of papers, and I'll look through these..." she said, her words trailing off as she noticed a thin, metal lever of sorts that had a slight curve to it.

As Rose looked through her stack of papers, Tara picked up the lever-like thing and studied its surface; there, at its thinnest point was the smallest smudged streak of wood polish. She looked back at the wardrobe, then back down at the lever. She walked over to the wardrobe, kneeling down and running her fingers around the edges where the sides met the base, until she found a near imperceptible indent one could easily overlook as a slight warping of the wood.

"Found something?" Rose asked, though Tara did not reply.

Instead, she positioned the lever, thinnest end first, into the indent, the curve facing inwards, and pushed it against the side of the wardrobe. As she did, the base began to lift, and she grabbed it and pulled it up to one side.

"Well, I guess we were both right, in a way" Rose said, now standing at her side and looking at the evidence before them "We should take this to Val'Ur straight away."

"Agreed."

***

Hamurfel, eastern route to the Royal Tombs

Ji'Roh could feel his lungs drying out as he ran, his heartbeat all he could hear in his ears. He wasn't sure if he had managed to outmanoeuvre Nor'un's guardsmen, the thunder of their horse's hooves still echoing in his mind, even if he couldn't actually hear them. But he wasn't about to stop and find out, and so continued his marathon run towards the royal tombs and the great obelisk that marked them, eager to make it home to his beloved Rose and ensure the King's sacrifice would not be in vein. He could see a dust storm coming in from the south, and knew it would be painful without the proper protection for his face, but was glad of it, for it would help shield him from the guardsmen and cover his tracks; all he needed to do was to keep moving, no matter how much his body ached, no matter the pain, he had to make it home.

***

Chancellor's Palace, Ebo

Val'Ur and Sierra rummaged through Lord Tallon's chamber, Sierra searching his bathing suite – which was in a separate but adjoining room – as Val'Ur went through a ledger of Tallon's she had found in his bedside cabinet, having broken its tiny lock with ease.

"So you and that Hamurfelion, you two are an item?" Val'Ur asked as she skimmed through the ledger's pages.

Sierra hesitated a moment, unsure of how to respond or react to such a question coming from a member off the Chancellery.

"Yes, yes m'lady, that we are" she replied finally, now looking through mirrored cupboards on the bathing suite's far side "It...we...it is strange how the fates threw us together."

Val'Ur gave a slight laugh.

"A patrolling warrior falling for an agent of the enemy King, yes, it is quite strange...but poetic"-she scanned down one of the ledger's pages relating to his finances-"Not that I'm one to judge; I am engaged to the King's sister after all."

Sierra paused her search a moment; she had forgotten – amongst all the chaoticness of wartime and her and Tara's journey – that the Chancellor's daughter had been engaged to the True Queen, and now she felt most sorry for her as she realised how long they had been kept apart.

"I'm sorry m'lady" she said as she walked over to the doorway, leaning upon its frame.

"Whatever for?" Val'Ur asked absently, still studying the same page.

"I...I cannot begin to imagine the pain this forced distance between you two must be causing."

Val'Ur looked up from the ledger briefly, looking over at Sierra and offering her a half smile of thanks for her concern, before returning her gaze to the journal.

"I think we may have something here..."-Sierra walked over to her, looking at where Val was pointing on the page-"but without something more concrete it's not enough, that's for sure."

"I don't understand" Sierra said, brow furrowed "how would such a purchase indicate corruption?"

"A sum that large is suspicious, especially for a Lord infamous for his tightfistedness; don't suppose you recognise the name of the recipient?" she asked "It's not a name I'm familiar with."

"Dredric Kor'ut...I feel like I have, but I can't place it" Sierra rubbed her chin thoughtfully "definitely feels like I should know it."

Just then they heard the sound of heavy footsteps echoing down the hallway outside.

"Tallon – he must have left the meeting early" Val whispered, hastily looking around the room "You hide in the bathing suite, quickly!"

"But what about you?"

"I'll be fine, trust me" she pushed the ledger into Sierra's hands "Now hide!"

***

The Royal Tombs, Hamurfel

Ji'Roh panted for what air he could take in, now slumped against a craggy nestle of rocks. He had made it to the Tombs, having passed by the great and towering obelisk that marked it ten minutes prior; it had stood out even as the dust storm overtook him, its monolithic structure dominating what visibility there had been. The storm still raged around him, but the weathered boulders he sat amongst gave him a small shelter that obscured the flow of sand and grit, helping save him from being choked by it, even with his lungs dried up and thirsting after such exertion. He hoped that the storm had thrown Nor'un's men off his trail, that it would give him time and opportunity to make his way south to the King's Generals and hopefully put an end to this war, and Nor'un's ambitions.

***

Chancellor's Palace, Ebo

Sierra had only just managed to hide around the doorframe of the bathing suit before Lord Tallon had entered the room. She could almost swear she heard him stop in shock as he realised Val'Ur was in his room.

"Val'Ur, what are you doing here?" he asked insistently, too distracted by her presence to notice the minor disruption they had caused to his room.

"My father sent me" she said confidently.

“...Did he now...interesting” he rubbed his chin unnervingly, his pudgy fingers jostling his folds of fat “Did he mention why?”

There was an even more unnerving manner in which he spoke that sent a shiver through Sierra’s spine; it sounded like excitement, the dark and terrible kind.

“He wished me to talk to you about your son, the General” Val’Ur trod lightly around the room’s central table “Perhaps we should talk someplace more formal?”

“No, here is fine” Tallon smiled sickeningly at her as he took a seat “Come child, sit on my lap and tell me what you need tell.”

“I beg your pardon?” Val’Ur froze in shock at the request.

“Sit” he said patting his bloated lap, his voice audibly more stern.

“Lord Tallon, must I remind you how improper such a proposition is? And that I am the Chancellor’s daughter?” she asked, hoping that it would be enough to dissuade him.

He rose to his podgy feet, visibly angered by her rejection.

“You are to wed my son Lady Ur, and I must make sure you are well suited to his needs.”

Val’Ur moved to exit the room, but Tallon blocked her path.

“Lord Tallon I really must insist you cease this disrespectful and repugnant behaviour” she said sternly and calmly.

“And I must insist that you allow me to try you out, my girl” he frowned.

“I am nobodies’ girl bar Amira’s!” she spat at him.

He made a grab for her, and instinctively she punched him with all the force she could bring right between the eyes, forcing him to stumble back and onto the floor.

"How many times have you tried that on those who couldn't fight back?" she snarled.

He got back to his feet, pulling out a dagger from his waist belt.

"Your father made a deal Lady Ur, and you were the price of my service; I will not be denied what is mine!" he shouted as he strode towards her.

Val'Ur brought up her fists, ready to pummel the obscene corruption of a man into submission, just as an ornate vase flew through the air in an arc that terminated against Tallon's head, shattering as it knocked him to the floor once more.

"Thought that'd be easier" Sierra said as she came up alongside Val'Ur "You alright?"

"I'm fine" she replied looking at the wailing Tallon at their feet "But he won't be" she stomped on his hand, forcing a scream from him.

"M'Lady, as much fun as it would be to see him suffer, surely it would be more useful to get him to talk?" Sierra asked, not sure whether to laugh or not at Tallon's pitiful state.

"Quite" Val'Ur agreed "What deal did you make with my father?" she asked, twisting her heal into his hand.

He yelped in pain, but gave no answer.

"Who is Dredric Kor'ut?" Sierra asked, but still he did not answer.

"Don't make me hurt you even more Tallon" Val'Ur warned, her face stone cold and vengeful.

"You really are a stupid woman aren't you?" he scoffed through his pain "Blind to how things really are!"

"All I have to do is send word of what you tried to do, and the people and your victims – yes, I know you've hurt others, for this came all to easily for you – will gather, and I will let them have you"-his eyes widened-"So I give you a choice: tell me everything and rot in a cell, or I let the people tear you limb from limb. Your choice."

He took a moment to weigh the options, before relenting to his selfish nature.

"Your father wants more war, and with it more profit."

"How do you play into that?"

"Dredric Kor'ut; he's a mercenary, an exiled Orc with his own men I use for my own ends."

"And that gets more war how exactly?" Sierra asked.

"They make fuel."

"Fuel? What are you talking about?"

"Vilwood."

"Vilwood? What of it?" Sierra asked

"You...you haven't heard?"

"No..." Val'Ur's expression changed, realising the truth, the last of the hope for her father shattered.

CHAPTER THIRTY-ONE

Palace of the Dred King Hamurfel

Aka Nor'un knelt beside the True Queen's bed, the Queen herself propped up by a large, singular pillow.

She did not know her brother had fallen two days prior, let alone to Nor'un's own blade. He was not cruel enough to tell her – or wise enough to know not to, depending on how one chose to look at it.

"So my brother has gone to the Orc Isles?" she asked him, still trusting of him in her ignorance of his actions.

"Indeed my Queen" he confirmed, building off of the Dred King's well intentioned white-lies with his own "He has gone to aid Val'Ur in their campaign – of which I'm sure he's told you all about."

She leaned back into her pillow, staying quiet as she thought.

"She is in no danger, is she Aka?"

"No, no" he comforted her "But it helps to have fresh eyes looking upon such things. Especially those who could be called an outsider to the situation."

"He did not say goodbye" she mused aloud, her voice as if she had been wounded by it "It...is so unlike him to do so."

"He did not want to pain you with a farewell, and the urgency of the situation also forced him depart with haste"-this was the hardest part of the lie-"Perhaps he wanted to spare his own heart; he does love you so dearly, and having to leave you whilst you are in this weakened state..."

The silence between them hung weightily as a servant brought her some water, and he wondered – worried – if he had convinced her.

"Perhaps"-she looked at him-"At least you are here...did you say Xürr and Zara went with him?"

"Yes I did, my Queen" Nor'un nodded with an uncharacteristic smile "But don't you worry, me and my troops will keep you and Akiro safe"

She couldn't see it, but his smile was all teeth.

"General" one of Nor'un's Commanders greeted him as he left the True Queen's chamber "How is our Queen?"

"As well as can be expected" Nor'un replied as they walked the Palace halls "She is still in the dark over both the war and her brother."

The Commander took a moment to respond.

"Sir, if I may, some of the men have...reservations"-Nor'un said nothing, waiting for more to be said-"There is unease at holding the throne whilst the Queen-"

"Do they fear for her safety?" Nor'un's question was sharp, cutting.

"No, no of course not General" the Commander replied apologetically "It is just, they do not like the idea of lying to her, given the circumstances."

"She is in no health to take such news" Nor'un stopped, the Commander doing likewise "What we do we do for the good of all Hamurfelions – lies to the True Queen included – and when – when – she is well enough to lead us once more I will yield my authority gladly."

"The men will be glad to hear that."

"I'm sure they will" Nor'un stared at him, then returned to walking "Have we any news from the front lines?"

"Nothing I'm afraid. Even if they had sent a messenger before that Orc escaped us, they may have been lost in the sandstorm."

Nor'un clenched his fist at the reminder of Val'Ur's messenger escaping – and with the King's seal no less; a problem he could not fix, not now.

"How many do we have hunting him down?"

"Sir, it is unlikely he would have survived the storm-"

"How many?" Nor'un would not ask a third time.

"Six; we can spare two more from the Eastern Pass if you wish it."

"No; as much as I would like to see that Orc in our hands, we cannot throw our numbers around so readily"-he furrowed his brow-"We must build ourselves some reinforcements – carefully; have you got a sense of the feeling at the nearby villages?"

"Reports are tentative, sir" the Commander apologised "Despite what it is believed our"-he caught himself-"what the Dred King had ordered done to that Orcish village, many are still disgruntled by our actions."

Disgruntled; it almost made Nor'un laugh.

They came to the throne room doors, Nor'un putting a hand upon it.

"Give them time; they will see we are what's best for our people."

*

Nor'un surveyed the city and what could be seen of Akiro from one of the upper Palace windows. The sun began to set, the orange sunbeams caught upon the dust in the air.

He had been a brute – uncompromising, aggressive, violent and dealt out death to others without mercy or hesitation – as he rose through the ranks of the Hamurfelion military. He'd always win his fights, if not the battle, learning tactics and how to use other's own against them.

The Old King, father to the True Queen and Dred King, had never made him General, despite his record. Nor'un understood why; sometimes how you won was more important than winning itself. When the True Queen had become, rising to the throne in the wake of her father's passing, he had stayed a

Commander, but one with close ties to the would-be Dred King. It was not that she did not trust him – he was a lifelong friend of her brother after all, and one who had shown unwavering loyalty – but rather that she could see him for who he was – what he was.

Loyal.

Ruthless.

Uncompromising.

Dangerous.

She could see he would have no issue, no thought or care at sacrificing countless lives to achieve his goal – and not just that of their troops. Useful at the right times, in the right circumstances, but destructive all the same. In contrast, the True Queen valued life, peace; thus her words brought such with every utterance.

He had approached her, walking with her through the Palace as he made his case, passing all manner of mosaics as she listened in good faith. After he had finished she had asked him a question: how many had he lost, how many troops had he failed?

It was not a phrasing he was use to; he could not give her an answer.

Next she asked him how many non-combatants had perished in his extermination of the marauders in the Northern Plaines; again, he could give no answer.

He had tried to give some kind of answer, some retort – though it was more of an excuse – but she cut him off, answering for him, and the numbers left him silenced.

She hadn't chastised him, didn't shout nor condescend, merely watching his reaction.

He looked to his feet in shame, and she placed a hand upon his shoulder, asking him – telling him – to learn. He was brilliant in his own way, but blind to that which he had not yet seen, or chosen not to see.

Years later, when the True Queen had first fallen ill and not that long after, when the Dred King had reluctantly taken the reins of the throne in her stead, Nor'un saw a chance.

He had waited for the Dred King to call on him for counsel, and gave it readily. Once that advice had proven itself true, Nor'un asked once more.

The Dred King listened.

A month after, General Nor'un was in command of a small garrison of troops – a compromise he had proposed himself, so he might prove his worthiness.

When the True Queen found out, she had summoned him to her chamber.

She didn't need to ask her question.

As he knelt beside her bed, he spoke on what he had learned. She asked him of his bloodlust, and he paused.

"I am what I am" he had answered "But I am no longer blind – war, fighting, these things need to be ended, prevented – and I now understand the cost of loss."-she had raised a weak eyebrow at that, and he had almost laughed-"I know I am made to kill, built for slaughter – I am very good at it –so why not make use of me, make me the sword to Zara's shield and aim me at those that would bring war and violence?"

He had liked that phrasing – Sword of Akiro, Sword of Hamurfel – though he was unsure if she had.

Perhaps it would have been different if she had recovered; what if she never did?

Nor'un looked down at his dagger, sheathed safely in his waistbelt. Upon its hilt read 'Aka, First of Sands' – a name given to him by his father when he was young and would steal figs from his father's trees, not unlike the sandstorms would.

He rested his hand upon it.

The blade had been a gift, received when he had become a Commander; not from his father – he had passed away many summers before then – but from his friend.

His friend.

Aka Nor'un, the friendless. That was how he felt now – who he was now.

He had never felt remorse from killing anyone – ever – so when it came to the Dred King...

Nor'un's finger tapped against the sheath.

He couldn't allow the Dred King to escape, couldn't risk him attempting to escape again; this he told himself.

The sun sunk deeper into the horizon.

He could have crippled him, removed his legs – no, he deserved better than that, deserved an honourable end.

Nor'un tilted his head, watching a handful of his men patrol the outside of the Palace grounds.

The True Queen had asked him to learn, and he had. The cost of war. The price of loss. It was why he had done what he had done.

Selling out Xürr's troop movements, taking the throne – killing his friend, his King; all in an effort to be...to be...

"Something more" he muttered to himself in a whisper "I should be something more."

More than a sword, more than a weapon to be let loose upon hapless foes.

He had tried so hard to become more than that. But a life lived as a blade leaves you cutting, makes you solve problems like they were all just flesh and armour.

He watched the city torches be lit as the sun finally disappeared, watched as their glow illuminated the dark and the sands within, then turned on his heel.

As he walked, his hand still upon the dagger's hilt, he felt something new – new to him at least. The True Queen would find out what he had done eventually – so long as she recovered from her illness – and what would she say then? Would she see? Would she see what he's done, and why he had done so?

He turned a corner, passing a servant carrying freshly cleaned linens down to the lower floors.

He had much planning to do.

Another corner, and another concern entered his mind; what if Amira never recovered?

What if her illness claimed her life?

All that power would rest in his hands, forever.

Nor'un was not one for power, not in that way. He wondered whether anyone would believe she passed naturally in that circumstance, or simply think he had brought her end himself.

He pondered – wondered – whether she would see he had not sacrificed numbers of their troops, their people – Dred King included – thoughtlessly. He had calculated each loss, each pain from each life extinguished, and found the ends made them worth it.

He entered his chambers, leaning upon his chair with his free hand.

The Dred King was gone.

His friend was gone.

Nor'un's grip on his dagger tightened.

He had never lost a fight. Never.

He did not feel the loss of others.

The True Queen, Amira, had asked him to learn, and he had thought he had.

Now he knew, knew he hadn't until now.

*

"Do we lie to her?" Kalib asked Samara as they ate their evening meal in their quarters, which was now locked and guarded by two of Nor'un's men.

Samara fidgeted with a dried fig as she wiped the last drops of moister from her plate with the dry, sandy bread in her left hand; she was missing home and its less bland food, amongst other things.

"I'm not sure" she said after a moment or two "the King had been rather specific in not upsetting her, and in her condition I'm sympathetic to his decision, but now he's gone…"-she took a bite of the bread, lightly chewing as its moistened but still rough texture rubbed her gums-"Now I'm not so sure; who knows if it would be safe for her if we did so."

"Right" Kalib nodded, looking back down at his plate and the food he had barely touched, rubbing the side of his neck in a subconscious act of anxiety; it goes almost without saying that this was not something either of them were used to.

Whilst they were arguably the most qualified and knowledgeable physicians in all the land, and as such had been called to all manner of places to treat all kinds of aliments, to be held prisoner – let alone by the usurper to the one who had hired them – was a new and unpleasant experience. What made it worse was that no-one in Blackwood would think anything of their absence, as they had mentioned to those that would otherwise worry that their work in Hamurfel would keep them away for an unspecified amount of time.

"Kalib, we'll be okay" Samara reassured him "It would not pay Nor'un to execute us; we're too well respected by powerful people."

"So was the Dred King."

"True, but he seems to want Amira – the True Queen – to get better, at least for now, so he needs us"-she put her fig back on her plate, and let out a sigh "I...for a moment I was so sure the King would get away..."

Kalib placed his hand on the side of her arm comfortingly.

"You did what you could Samara, no one else I know could have done more. At least the messenger managed to escape"-he moved back to his plate, pushing his food around it with a fork- "You think the Orcs will help the Hamurfelions once he tells them what has happened?"

“I hope so” she said, pouring some water into a dulled silver goblet “But he has to make it to them first, and no doubt Nor’un will be sending men after him.”

They sat in silence a while, the room quiet save for the sound of Kalib scraping his plate every now and then, Samara leaning back into her chair as she tried to quell her thoughts.

Suddenly their door began to unlock, then open, one of the guards entering the room with one hand on the hilt of his sword.

“King Nor’un wishes to discuss True Queen Amira’s treatment” the man said, waiting impatiently for them to follow him.

The pair looked at each other silently, kalbi looking regretfully down at the still half-full plate before him.

“Guess I’ll have to finish this later” he mumbled to himself as they rose from their seats.

CHAPTER THIRTY-TWO

Ebo, Capital City of the Orc Isles Council Chamber, two days since Tallon's capture

"My daughter, what is the meaning of this?" Korren'Ur asked as he walked into the Council chambers.

Around the room's central table sat almost two thirds of the Lords, Val'Ur siting at the head of the table where her father would sit, Sierra and Tara standing either side of her. As he looked around them he notice the missing Lords, realising quickly they were – like Lord Tallon – those he had arrangements with.

"We know what you've done Korren" she said coldly, her expression emotionless "And we will not allow you to bastardise our people or our honour any longer."

"You dare be so disrespectful as to address me, your father, by my first name?"

"I dare" she said dryly "I have informed the Lords of your schemes."

"Oh? Schemes is it? And what proof do you have of such things?" he asked dismissively "I knew you were unkeen to marry Lord Tallon's son, but this-".

With that Sierra threw down Tallon's ledger, and more importantly, Korren's writs and letters of blackmail he had hidden away beneath his wardrobe's base panel; every filthy secret he thought he could hold onto was laid bare upon the great stone table, and all he thought he could use to further his own ends now being used against him instead.

"These are clearly forgeries" he attempted to wave it off.

"No they are not, Korren" one of the Lords shouted "We have checked, and we have the confession of ex-Lord Tallon."

Korren looked from one Lord to the next, finally resting his gaze upon his daughter.

"Why?" he asked her as if the others were not present.

"I am not yours to give."

He nodded slowly, calmly.

"So, there is no recourse? No means of persuading you otherwise?" he asked, all of them staring silently back at him "Then I guess I have no choice. Guards?"

Val realised what was about to happen, rising from her seat and unsheathing her ceremonial blade – Soulbreaker – as fast as she could, but it was not fast enough.

"Imprison these fools" Korren said dryly, his tone that of disappointment as his loyalists stormed in behind him and began dragging the uncorrupted Lords out of the chamber as they shouted to be released. Sierra and Tara readied themselves either side of Val'Ur, the three of them unwilling to go down without a fight.

Just as Korren's Loyalists moved to engage, echoes of thundering hooves and metal clad footsteps came up the side of the mountain, up from its base and the hollows within, the city roaring like a spooked beast. Val turn to look through the chamber's stained-glass window, recognising the banners flying high as they ascended the mountain, and felt a smile of relief come over her; it was Kaymar, who – true to his word – had come to aid her. She turned back to the loyalists.

"General Kaymar, son of Lord Kaymar, comes to Ebo's aid. If you lay down your weapons, and release the good Lords from their false imprisonment, then we shall be merciful; if not? I will end you traitorous thugs myself!" she seethed confidently and loudly, the loyalists looking between each other as they tried to form a silent consensus amongst themselves "Well? What say you all?"

There was a series of metal clangs as swords fell to the obsidian floor, the loyalist realising, quite sensibly, that they were outmatched and outnumbered by Kaymar's warriors. And with that the three ladies let out a muted sigh of relief; now all they needed was to capture Korren and make peace with the Hamurfelions.

CHAPTER THIRTY-THREE

Cairngor, Disputed Lands

Xürr fended off an Orcish greatsword amid the clash of blade and metal; it was a small skirmish – a light testing of their defensive line – but that did not make it any less important.

He had followed Rahool into battle, something a General would not normally do outside of larger, more important engagements, but he had need of releasing his frustrations upon something – and with Nor'un beyond his grasp the Orcs would have to suffice.

Rahool cut down Xürr's attacker with ease, granting the Orc a swift end, and the two surveyed the relatively sparse fighting going on around them.

"Zara will not be please with you" Rahool commented without an ounce of judgment in his voice.

"She'll forgive me" Xürr replied as he leaned upon his sword "She too feels the frustration of our situation."-he straightened himself up a little, looking about to see if he was needed in the ongoing brawl-"I'm surprised you didn't insist upon using your horses on this lot."

"Not worthy enough of a fight" he replied, eyeing three Orcs hacking at two of his men as the other Warriors retreated "I'll handle these three; you head back to Zara."

With that, Rahool strode away towards them at a speed disproportionate to his size.

Xürr smirked, resting his sword upon his shoulder as he turned and headed back to the tents.

Zara watched the skirmish from afar, thinking on what good it would do to chastise Xürr for being so reckless; if he fell in battle she would be left to command their troops against the Orcs – and Nor'un, when it came to it– all by herself. Her hands grasped tightly, if fidgetively, to her horse's reins; she had been inspecting the whole of their defensive line, checking on troop positioning first-hand and talking to her Second Commanders, and despite their high moral and firm hold on their half of Cairngor it had left her nervous. Not for Xürr – now walking his way to her – or even their ability to keep the Orcs at bay, but for the bigger threat to Hamurfel. They had lost – and were losing –

numbers of troops to maimings and death that mirrored the Orcs's losses, enough to make even the thought of needing to liberate Akiro from Nor'un deeply unsettling. If Nor'un was to move against the Dred King, and she were forced to retreat homeward to put a stop to his ambitions, it would mean abandoning – losing – Cairngor to the Orcs, or choosing to abandon Akiro to hold Cairngor; they did not have the numbers to save both. Either way Hamurfel would lose, but if Nor'un took Akiro, all of Hamurfel would fall under his thrall shortly thereafter – even if the people rebelled, he would have the True Queen as his hostage, and no true Hamurfelion would risk her, no matter the cost.

"You needn't have joined that skirmish" she said bluntly to Xürr as he walked up beside her, the pair of them beginning to move back towards their camp; he just gave a light shrug in response "Come, our chief physician needs a word with us."

Coming from north of the Hamurfelion forces, Ji'Roh walked, bloodied and exhausted, towards the Hamurfelion camp. He had escaped capture, bandits and the odd hungry predator, but now he was within reach of his last destination before he could head home to Ebo and to his dear, beloved Roselia.

CHAPTER THIRTY-FOUR

Ebo, Capital City of the Orc Isles

Taymar moved with purpose, and having sent a few of his best men to secure his father's safety, made his way towards the Council Chamber. He had long carried a guilt that weighed him down, and had felt a coward for not having intervened in the affairs of the Orcish Lords sooner; but then he had not known the full extent of their duplicitous and corrupt actions, let alone the Chancellor's betrayal of the people; and to his great shame, he had not thought he would find support in his friend Val'Ur until he had received her request for aid. His inaction over Vilwood weighed heavily upon him – the lives of the people, of all those families, the massacre of their lives and history, felt like a stain upon his soul that would haunt him until his final days – but, if he could help bring those responsible to justice, help Val'Ur bring an end to the war and bloodshed, here and now, perhaps...perhaps that would be enough.

"Sir, we've secured the main Council Chamber" one of his vanguard said as he rushed down the obsidian steps.

"What of Val'Ur? The Chancellor?" Kaymar asked, nervous of the reaction the Chancellor and his corrupted Lords would take.

"Val'Ur is safe in the Council Chamber, but the Chancellor eludes us"

"What of the Lords?"

"The ones on your arrest list are being protected by loyalist guards, sir" the warrior wiped his brow "We fear they hold the others for ransom."

"Damn!" Kaymar muttered "Take me to Val'Ur, and send word to our men to hold position; we want as little bloodshed as possible, so use our numbers to intimidate them into staying put."

The warrior nodded, ordering two of his subordinates to carry the message to the others, then turning on the spot to lead Kaymar onward.

CHAPTER THIRTY-FIVE

Cairngor Disputed Lands

Ji'Roh stumbled forward, taking care to hold his hands high above his head. Strangely – or so he thought – he felt more scared now than when Nor'un had almost caught him and killed the Hamurfelion King; here he was on a battlefield, on what was in principle the 'enemy's side' of the conflict, where he could easily be seen as a combatant or spy.

He slowly approached two Hamurfelion soldiers as they packed provisions to take further down the line.

"E-Excuses me" Ji'Roh called out tentatively, the two soldiers turning to face him, unsheathing their swords hastily once they realised he was an Orc "I carry a message for General Zara from the Chancellor-in-waiting Val'Ur."

He hoped they believed him as they weighed him and his words up, exchanging quiet glances with one another.

"Do not move" one of them said sternly, pacing over to him swiftly.

"Sure" Ji'Roh agreed, his every muscle tense with nervousness.

The soldier patted him over, checking for any concealed weapons.

"Okay; he's unarmed" the Hamurfelion called back to the other, before staring Ji'Roh square in the eyes "You do *exactly* what we say, when we say it" she said harshly, shoving him forward lightly, not that he minded; he was just glad they believed him, or were at least curious.

*

Rahool walked into Zara's war-tent, where she and Xürr were going over the latest casualties with their chief physician.

"I require a private talk with the Generals" he boomed at the doctor, who humbly excused himself, ducking past Rahool as he left the tent.

"What is it Rahool?" Zara asked, her voice weary from the struggles of war.

"An Orc has handed himself over to us."

"Is that so strange?" Xürr asked "We have beaten them back at every turn these last few weeks; about time they started to surrender."

"He came from *behind* our lines."

"Now that changes things" Zara said, this new detail making her suddenly alert.

"More than you know General; he claims to have news on Nor'un and a missive from none other than Val'Ur herself."

Zara and Xürr looked at each other, disbelieving, then back at Rahool.

"Can we trust him?" asked Xürr as he folded his arms.

"He had this, and said the King himself ordered it delivered to you" Rahool produced the King's seal from his pocket as he spoke, handing it to Zara.

She felt her legs go weak, almost stumbling back as her body forced her to take a seat at the sight of it.

"He...my word...no, No this cannot be!" she exclaimed, knowing what it meant.

"The King's seal...does this mean-?" Xürr asked looking upon the signet ring in Zara's hands, Rahool interrupting him with an answer before he could finish.

"Yes, it would seem so" he sighed sombrely "but we have this Orcish messenger, and with him perhaps a chance to end this war, and Nor'un, with any luck."

"I...I just cannot believe he...he actually did it..." Zara said, almost absent from the conversation.

"Bring the Orc here Rahool; let us hear his words for ourselves" Xürr ordered, starting to make the beginnings of plans in his head.

Rahool gave a courteous nod before departing to fetch Ji'Roh as quickly as possible. Xürr looked to Zara, concern evident upon his face.

"You don't think he would have hurt the True Queen, do you?"

Zara looked up from the signet ring, still dumbstruck by the loss of her King and the shame of having failed him.

"I – No, no Nor'un is many things, but he is not stupid; the people might tolerate the loss of the King, but the True Queen? They would all rather die fighting than live under him then."

"True" Xürr nodded "But what if she succumbs to her illness?"

Zara paused a moment, having not thought of that.

"Let us hope that does not happen; at least not until Nor'un is ousted."

CHAPTER THIRTY-SIX

Council Chamber, Chancellor's Palace Ebo

"Kaymar" Val'Ur greeted him with a nod as he entered the room, relieved her friend had reached her in time "I was glad to hear you got my message; I am even more thankful for the timing of your arrival."

"It would seem I got here not a moment too soon"-he sheathed his sword for the time being-"Your messenger, did he make it to Hamurfel?"

"We do not know; he has yet to return"-she gestured to Tara-"But the Dred King sent one of his own to me, and by his words we are already agreed."

There was a brief pause, the sounds of Kaymar's warriors and guardsmen securing the Chancellor's Palace in the background.

"So the war is over?" he asked at last, daring to hope.

"In principle, yes; but we must make it to the front lines before it truly is."

"Right."

Sierra stepped forward, politely bowing as she entered the conversation.

"General. Chancellor." She began "What of Korren'Ur and his loyalists? They still hold most of the Lords hostage."

"Father might be tempted to flee, or bargain for such an escape from the consequences of his actions" Val'Ur mused "Perhaps we can persuade his men to change their minds and leave his side?"

"Do they know of Vilwood?" Kaymar asked, sorrow noticeably entering his eyes "of what Lord Tallon had..." he paused, chocked by guilt as he saw Val'Ur knew of what he spoke "Val, I could not stop it, not without surrendering Ebo to-"

"There will come time for redemption Kay" she interrupted him, putting a hand upon his shoulder "You are my friend – I know you; if there had been anyway you could have stopped it you would have."-she paused for but a moment-"But as for his loyalists, it is a good question if they know."

"Perhaps they do not, and it could persuade them that theirs is not a cause worth dying for."

It was worth a shot, so Val'Ur thought.

She turned back to Sierra and Tara.

"Sierra, Tara, I know you both want nothing more than to move on to your new life together, but I must ask of you one more thing, for the good all our people."

"What is it you ask of us?" Tara asked.

"I need you both to ride with me to the disputed lands in Cairngor, so that you, trusted messenger of the Hamurfelion Court, might show your Generals your King's words as you did for me. Together, we will show them the corruption that had infected us, and my warriors will heed my words as I tell them how my father framed the Hamurfelions for the Vilwood massacre."

"Well?" Sierra asked Tara.

She took the briefest moment to think it over.

"All right; for peace, and the True Queen."

"But first" Val'Ur turned to Kaymar "we must deal with my father."

Kaymar's warriors stood to the side as he and Val'Ur walked towards the iron door her father had barricaded himself behind; he had tried to flee, but every which way he turned he had found Kaymar's warriors blocking his path.

"Father!" Val'Ur banged on the ancient door to the Hall of Remembrance "You have lost, save yourself this indignity and surrender yourself!"

"My men have your Lords daughter, held hostage to my demands; you have no place to bargain" came his voice, angry and desperate.

"Actually, they don't"-she could almost hear his despair as she spoke-"Once we told them what you did – what you had Lord Tallon do – most gave up, sickened by who they had been defending. Those few who still saw you as Chancellor are no more, and the real Lords stand with me. You have no allies. No warriors. Just this metal door between you and me."

There was silence.

Val'Ur knew he would be thinking desperately for a way out of where he found himself, that he'd try to bargain or manipulate her; the only question was which tactic he'd use.

"You know I will be executed Val? Would you do that, allow your own father to be beheaded like some common thug?"

There it was; manipulation.

She took a deep breath.

"You caused the deaths – the butchering - of almost forty families; do you not deserve such a fate?"-she took a breath, and steadied herself emotionally-"You ceased to be the man who raised me long ago. He is dead, and all I have left is you, a ghoul that isn't even a shadow of what he was."-she looked back at Kaymar, who gave her a nod of reassurance-"If you surrender now you will receive a fair trial, and a fair judgment. You will not be harmed, nor abused; this dignity I offer you in the name of the man you once were."

Silence once more came the reply as she waited for his response; it felt like an eternity.

Kaymar moved to order his men to break down the door, but Val'Ur raised her hand, silently ordering him to wait, and he did so.

Another moment of silence.

Then came the sound of the door's ancient locks opening.

*

Warriors bustled around Tara, making quick and speedy preparations for the journey to Cairngor. She was nervous as she unfurled her headscarf, taking a moment to look upon it. It wasn't a fanciful thing, not grand or adorned with golden silk threads, but it was special. She put it on as Sierra brought over their horses.

"You ready?" she asked as she handed Tara the reins to her horse, her eyes noticeably distracted by the headscarf.

"It felt like it was the right moment to put it on"-Tara answered the unasked question first-"seeing as I no longer need hide the fact I'm Hamurfelion. And yes, I'm ready."

Sierra gave her a nod of understanding as she helped Tara up onto her horse – she didn't need to, but she wanted to – before jumping up upon her own.

"If it makes you happy" Sierra said, replying to Tara's explanation. There was something in her voice, not bad, not negative really, but more of an unasked question or withheld opinion; Tara left it be regardless.

*

Kaymar walked with Val'Ur down the mountain's exterior steps, their meeting with the remaining Lords having gone as smoothly as it could given the circumstances.

"Are you sure you must be the one to go?" he asked her, and not for the first time "You have just claimed the Chancellery, and the Lords are still shaken...the people will be unsettled."

"They already are, Kaymar" her voce was sombre, if hopeful "But I hear your concerns."-a few steps passed, the sound of a city in dismay loud in the air-"I must go, I assure you; my presence upon the battlefield is something neither side can ignore, and thus the quickest way to ensure a peaceful end to this bloodied affair."

"And if the people revolt, thinking you've abandoned them?"

She looked at him.

"You think they would?"

He was quiet a moment, sucking his lips in thought.

"It is unlikely, I confess, but it is not outside the bounds of possibility."

"I trust you'll be able to calm their worries" she smiled "You trust the remaining Lords? That they will hold true to their word?"

"Some more than others, but no serious doubt" he paused "Val, are you sure I should not go in your stead?"

"Quite sure" she gave a confident smile "I need you here, watching things, maintaining order, whilst I...I must ensure peace."

"You wish to see Amira again"-he stepped to the side to let a servant pass-"I understand. I promise you, Ebo will not fall to chaos in your absence."

They walked in silence a while, almost at the mountain's base now.

"My father, his trial, could you wait on it until my return?" she asked of him.

"I can try, line up the Lords who aided his schemes first, move focus to hunting down the butcher Dredric for a while, but if the people grow...restless, I will not have much of a choice."

She looked out at Ebo's sprawling mass radiating out from the mountain like a shining obsidian spiderweb, thinking upon its people – her people.

"How could he betray so many?" she found herself asking aloud; Kaymar wasn't sure how to answer.

"It would seem greed got the better of him" he said after a moment "But betraying strangers – even those you are sworn to protect – is an easy turn once you've betrayed your own kin."

"Indeed."

"Val, you mentioned in your letter...did Tallon or his son...did they...*touch* you?"

Val'Ur stopped in her tracks, Kaymar doing likewise, waiting patiently as she stood quiet.

"Tallon tried; I knocked him to the ground" she answered at last as she returned to walking.

"Good" he nodded "Perhaps his trial will be first."-he forced a laugh, but Val'Ur didn't-"What of his son though? Given your father's plans and what you said in the letter...?"

Val'Ur stayed silent, her gaze frozen to where she was walking.

"...I see." Kaymar understood what her silence meant, though he kept his anger hidden; she did not need to be burdened with his feelings about what happened also "I don't wish to distress you with the memory, but, if I may ask – as your friend – how, what did...?"

She didn't answer, not at first.

"I am strong Kaymar, physically equal to any warrior"-he stayed quiet, listening compassionately as she searched for the words she needed-"Tallon found that out the hard way via my fist, so...why..."-she gave a heavy breath-"It could have been so much worse, he didn't...I should have fought him off harder, sooner."

Kaymar fumed internally, but outwardly he placed a hand upon the back of Val'Ur's shoulder.

"Don't blame yourself Val, never"-she looked at him-"Their actions are theirs and theirs alone."

They were almost with the warriors now, just a few turns around the obsidian walls.

"When did he...?" Kaymar couldn't find the words "Was it more than once?"

"Only once"-she paused-"though he tried a few more times when I was alone and away from Rose."-she held back, stopping where she stood, putting her head in her hand-"He forced his tongue into my mouth Kay, and no amount of whiskey could wash out the, the...just thinking about it makes me feel unclean."

Kaymar turned to her fully, putting his hands upon her shoulders, looking her square in the eyes.

"Was that all?"-he pause, his voice soft-"Or would you rather we stop this conversation?"

"If you mean...no, no other...part...was forced...inside me"-she felt sick remembering it, her stomach churning heavily-"not that he didn't try...by the divines, I'm so strong, trained for war and combat, can fight off any man or beast, and yet...yet I couldn't fight – why?" she stifled her voice, uneasy at the chance others would hear her-"He grabbed me, you know? I...I had to make an excuse, to act and say we should wait, wait until we were wed, anything to get him off me"-Kaymar felt helpless seeing her pain-"Why couldn't I fight Kay? Why couldn't I fight back? It, it was as if I couldn't move, like I was paralyzed, none of my muscles could move as I wanted them to, I...it was like...I was screaming at myself to move, to fight, and I just...I just couldn't"-she let out a frustrated sigh-"That was when I knew I couldn't let the damned war go on, that I finally accepted I had to stand against my father."

Kaymar realised just how long she had lived with this burden, how long she had to endure the pain in silence.

"Val, you're right – you are strong. Perhaps the strongest there is. But, attacks such as those, they don't play the same as combat"-she looked up at him, away from the distressing memory-"So hear my words and know they are true: it was NOT your fault. You *are* strong. The fact you couldn't fight back does not mean you are weak or somehow deserving of what happened – it makes you mortal, like everyone else. Things such as these, they are shocking, abhorrent, and such a violation to one's being, that it's almost impossible to fight back; no normal mind can comprehend or cope with it as it happens."-he wasn't sure if his words were helping or just making things worse for her, but he felt compelled to try-"Val, I...would you like me to hurt him?"

She looked into his eyes intently.

"You would do that for me? Sully your honour?"

"I would follow you into the voids of Oblivion Val'Ur, march by your side as you confronted insurmountable odds and death itself. You are my friend, and I will do right by you, always."

She put her hand upon his, and gave a strong, if weary smile.

"The offer is appreciated, truly, but he is beneath you – beneath me. He will have his trial, and he will hang"-she paused-"But...I do not want people to know what he did to me."

"Why not? There could be others-"

"Then we say he assaulted a lady, we say what he did but not to whom."

"Val..."

"I will not be seen as a victim...If Amira ever found out, I fear it would break her heart, and her health is too fragile to be able to weather such things..."

"I...I understand" he nodded, accepting her decision; but he would make sure the noose for Tallon's son would hurt; his was not going to be a quick death "I'm, I'm so sorry I wasn't there Val, if-"

"Don't go apologising now Kay" she stopped him, straightening herself up, putting effort into regaining her composure for when she walked amongst her warriors "the last thing I need is to start crying over your friendship and have my face-paint smear."

She was trying to be humorous in the face of it all, and Kaymar felt in awe of her strength; she was stronger than he would have been, so he thought.

"If ever you need to talk" he offered as they began to walk once more.

"Thank you" she gave him a light nudge with her shoulder "but Rose has been my rock, even in her rather pregnant state – you look after her whilst I'm away, okay?"

"You have my word."

They now stood before the warriors, whom were all but ready to leave for Cairngor. She turned to him.

"I trust you to keep the peace Kaymar; there is no-one else I'd entrust such a task bar you"-she leaned in to whisper-"and please, make sure I never see any hint of Tallon or his son ever again."

"I can promise you that Val, or should I say Chancellor?"

'Chancellor Val'Ur, Guardian of the Orc Isles'; it had a nice ring to it, so she thought.

"Only in official settings my friend" she smiled "And I can give you my word, next time we meet, there will be peace between us and the Hamurfelions."

Whilst Val'Ur was away, Tallon and his son had their trials and were found guilty on all counts, to no-one's surprise. They died a terrible death, but one well deserved.

*

They were now halfway back to Cairngor, and had made camp outside one of the small taverns Sierra and Tara had passed on their way to Ebo; Val'Ur had use of the rooms whilst the warriors made do in their tents – Sierra and Tara allowed a small, cupboard like room; something of a gift from Val'Ur, for she saw much of her and Amira in them.

Since they had left Ebo Tara had been wearing her headscarf, at first it had been only whilst they travelled, but now it was most of the time; Sierra wasn't sure what to make of it.

"Tara" she asked as she watched her carefully remove it and place it upon her satchel "why do you wear that headscarf?"

Tara gave a side glance, eyebrow raised in quiet question.

"You know Elisa gave it to me" she replied as she pushed herself up the bed that could barely hold one of them, let alone both.

"I understand – as I understand why you always wear her locket – but...why cover your hair? It is so beautiful."

Tara couldn't look at her a moment, until Sierra started stroking her hair, gently running her fingers through it; it was a nice feeling.

"I feel...vulnerable without it; when my hair is uncovered I feel naked and exposed before the world"-she closed her eyes and leaned into Sierra, lost in the feeling of Sierra's heartbeat, and her fingers drifting through her hair like a soft breeze-"It's not that I dislike it being uncovered, or won't, it's just – to me – it's an intimate thing."

Sierra stopped stroking her hair a moment; a brief pause as she thought.

"Is this a Hamurfelion thing?" she asked "A cultural exuberance you had to hide whilst you pretended to be of the Orc Isles?"

"No, yes; it is not as simple as that"-she looked up at Sierra-"Hamurfelion's wear headscarves because they're practical – our duststorms and sandstorms you see, and the heat – but it is not our way to feel as *I* feel."

Sierra thought on that a while.

"You say you feel vulnerable with your hair down, that the headscarf makes you feel safe?"-Tara nodded gently-"But, all the time I've known you, you've been so strong – remember those bandits that ambushed us?"

"I fear you miss the point, starlight."

Sierra gave a small smile at the nickname, and gently lifted Tara's head to face her, her mismatched emerald and sapphire eyes looking upon Tara with a deep love.

"Perhaps I do. Perhaps I'll never understand the mind-set you have about your hair, or perhaps I will. Maybe there'll come a time where you no longer feel the need to wear it, for you feel safe...with me"-Tara went to speak, but Sierra gently placed a finger upon her lips-"Tara, what I'm saying is, I'm with you regardless, and I understand now – if nothing else – that you letting me touch your hair so freely is a sign of trust and love."

Tara remained quiet a moment.

"Do you understand, or do you *think* you understand?"

"How would I know the difference?"

Tara turned on her back, allowing Sierra to caress her hair with both hands.

"Let's say you were a stranger, and you touched my hair as you do now, I would feel violated – a strong sentiment I know, but it is how I feel – and I would defend myself as such."-Sierra stayed quiet as she listened, feeling the soft waves in Tara's hair-"Sometimes I feel...envious of the other girls who wear their hair so freely, whom dress it however they like, but I do not – would not – want them to cover theirs; does that make sense?"

"I think so."

"I think"-Tara nestled against Sierra a little more-"that it's the way the cloth holds against the sides of my face and keeps my hair pressed against me like a bundled new-born."-she gave a pause-"And to tell an intimate truth, when I feel you caressing my hair-"

Sierra leaned over and kissed her on the forehead, interrupting her thoughts.

"Tara, do not feel like you need justify yourself to me; I love you for you. I am – was – just curious of this part of you I didn't understand. I still don't get it, not fully, but so long as it is of no harm to you I am more than fine with it; not that you need me to be fine with it."

Tara thought on that; could her headscarf cause her harm? Or was Sierra speaking of *why* she felt she needed to wear it?

"Well, you can be sure of one thing" she yawned as she pulled herself up against Sierra fully "*You* can touch my hair anytime, anyplace."

CHAPTER THIRTY-SEVEN

Front Lines, Cairngor, Disputed Lands

Rahool sat atop his trusty steed, itself adorned in its own ornate-yet-functional armour – arguably the most battle-ready horse in all the land that one – Zara at his side as he held the white flag of negotiation high above them; Xürr stayed back, probing Ji'Roh for all the information he could on Nor'un and his hold on Akiro.

They had ordered their soldiers to stand down and retreat a good fifty yards as a sign of good faith as they had first raised the flag, but that had been near half an hour ago now.

"They're taking their sweet time" Rahool muttered "Where's the respect?"

"You forget what our new friend has told us Rahool; to them we are butchers of children, slayers of non-combatants" Zara reminded him "They're probably debating whether or not to kill us where we stand."

"They wouldn't break the rules of combat."

"Why not?" Zara looked at him "They think we have."

Rahool kept staring at the enemy lines.

"They are Orc warriors; they are made of honour" he said after a quiet moment, before directing her attention with a nod "See?"

From the Orcish lines came two distinctly armoured Orcs – Generals, Rahool told Zara, judging by the blues on their pauldrons – flanked either side by two shield-bearing guards.

"Let's hope they listen" Zara said under her breath, mostly to herself, before the Orcs could come into earshot.

They came to a stop six yards in front of Rahool.

"You wish to open negotiations?" One of the General's asked.

"Yes" Zara replied "I am General Zara, this is Commander Rahool" she introduced them, sparing the Orcs her longer title.

"I am General Sira'Or" the other General introduced herself.

"And I am General Mozin'Ra" the first General added, his voice barely hiding his anger – or disgust – at his Hamurfelion counterparts "Perhaps you wish to surrender?"

Rahool resisted the urge to spit in his face – there was almost no greater dishonour to Rahool, other than disrespecting his horse, than suggesting he would flee from battle or surrender.

"No, not surrender" Zara replied calmly, shifting her gaze from the clearly disgruntled Rahool back to the Generals "But rather something more important."

"This is a waste of time" Mozin'Ra grunted, hot beneath his armour "These people are butchers."

"We are not butchers!" Rahool shouted.

"I think it best we hold our tongues, and hear what each other have to say" Sira'Or suggested "Then we decide where or if we unsheathe our rage."

"Agreed" Zara nodded, turning to Mozin'Ra "General, I can assure you no Hamurfelion partook in the butchering of Vilwood, on my oath."

"Then how do you know of it Hamurfelion?" he asked, clearly not believing her.

"We have a messenger, a trusted confidant sent by Val'Ur herself."-she let that sink in for but a fleeting moment-"He had been tasked to deliver a message to our King – one of peace and a request for aid."

Mozin'Ra raised an eyebrow, leaning back on his horse; that would be an oddly specific lie to tell.

"What is this messenger's name?" Sira'Or asked.

"His name?" Zara turned to Rahool "Rahool?"

"Ji'Roh" Rahool boomed "Say's he's husband to Val'Ur's personal maid."

"Handmaid" Zara corrected him.

The Orcish Generals exchanged looks.

"Do continue" Mozin'Ra urged them.

"He speaks of witnessing the Vilwood massacre, and the murder of our King"-that news visibly shocked the Orcs, for none knew the Dred King had fallen, or of Nor'un's betrayal-"Rahool, show them the scroll from Val'Ur."

Rahool pulled the scroll from his belt, handing it to Sira'Or, who hastily read through it.

"Well?" Mozin'Ra asked her.

"Most of this is written with...personal detail" she began "But if this is true – and I see no reason to doubt these words or her broken seal – then we have been betrayed."

"If the Hamurfelions did not butcher Vilwood, then who?" Mozin'Ra questioned.

"According to Ji'Roh, it was a band of Orcs" Rahool answered.

"Lies!"

"Do not impugn my honour, General" Rahool cautioned "I might be a brute of war, but I do not lie."

"We are not asking you to trust us" Zara interjected "We are asking – all we're asking – is that we call a truce, at least until we can verify Ji'Roh's account of the matter."

"That sounds reasonable enough" Sira'Or agreed, looking back down at Val'Ur's message "Mozin?"

"Aye...but I would like to speak with Ji'Roh" Mozin'Ra requested "If I feel his words hold true on Vilwood, you shall have your truce."

Rahool looked to Zara.

"Then we are agreed" Zara nodded "Rahool, if you could be so kind?"

"You would have me leave you unguarded?"

"With respect Commander" Sira'Or almost smiled "We can see your archers ready to take us out if we try anything; ours stand ready to do the same."

Rahool smiled; he liked this General – she thought the same way he did.

"Very well" he spoke boomingly "I shall return with Ji'Roh swiftly."

*

"I'm glad the talk of a truce holds true" Val'Ur remarked as she led her small army of Kaymar's warriors towards what had been the front lines.

"On that we are most agreed" Tara replied, she and Sierra riding next to her at her request "Perhaps your messenger reached my King."

Many of the Orcish warriors had come out of their tents to see Val'Ur, word of her arrival traveling fast through their ranks – her presence made obvious by the Chancellery banners being held aloft by flagbearers; both those on foot and on horseback – eager to see what she would say, how she would react to the current truce.

As she drew up to the edges of Orcish controlled ground, one of her foot-soldiers stepped forward and waved her banner in big, interloping arcs.

"You're known to the Hamurfelion Generals you say?" Val'Ur asked Tara.

"Yes Chancellor Ur; as one of the Dred King's personal messengers, I am well acquainted with his Generals and Commanders; most of his court, truth be told."

"Good; with luck we will have peace restored between our people before the end of evening" Val'Ur's voice was hopeful, and so was Sierra and Tara – for with peace would come their chance of a life together.

"Who is that?" Val'Ur asked; she was familiar with the Generals of Hamurfel by nature of her relationship with the True Queen, but she did not recognise the man riding towards them.

Tara shielded her eyes from the sun to get a better view of him.

"By the looks of it...Commander Rahool" she answered after a moment "A good man – made of honour – if a little brutish on the battlefield."

Val'Ur nodded in acknowledgement.

"Lady Ur, daughter of High Chancellor Korren'Ur of the Orc Isles?" Rahool asked as he drew up before them.

"Yes, though now it is Chancellor Val'Ur" Val'Ur replied "This truce, was it an order from your King?"

Rahool stared at her, thinking on what was, and was not, his place to say.

"Your Generals are talking to your messenger – Ji'Roh – as we speak"-there was a look of relief in Val'Ur's eyes-"I trust by your presence and title your father is no longer an issue?"

"In a way; there is much damage to fix and a few corrupt Lords who slipped away as we liberated our people who we need to hunt down"-she paused, seeing something in the look in his eyes-"Commander, you look at me with worry; what is it?"

"I think it best you hear it from your messenger, Chancellor" Rahool gestured to the Hamurfelions' main tent "The Generals of both sides are with him as we speak."

"Best we meet with them then" Val'Ur began riding towards the tent, her warriors following dutifully behind her.

"Messenger" Rahool greeted Tara with a bow of his head, choosing to ride beside her.

"Commander" she replied in kind "I hope we have not lost too many of our people."

"Or ours" Sierra added.

"That might be the least of our worries now" Rahool leaned close, talking in a whisper; she could see it in his eyes – something was very, very wrong.

"What's happened?" she whispered in turn, glancing at Val'Ur a few yards ahead of them as she quickly realised this was the news best broken to Val'Ur by Ji'Roh.

Rahool looked to Val'Ur, judging how quiet he needed to be, then whispered to her as he leaned as close as he could.

"The Dred King has fallen, murdered by Nor'un."

She could feel her spine freeze and her breath escape her with the shock of those words. She held herself together, not wanting this to be how Val'Ur learned this most heart-breaking news; Rahool had continued to talk, telling her of all she had missed and that had happened whilst she were in the Orcish lands, but she didn't hear a word – it was like deafening silence as she tried to wrap her mind around such a painful loss. She knew she couldn't have stopped it – even if she had been there, what could she have done? What if she had delivered the King's letter faster – could she have delivered it faster?

"What of the True Queen?" She asked in a hushed whisper as they drew close to the Hamurfelion tents.

"Safe, so far as we know" Rahool assured her "Nor'un isn't that stupid."

It was not long before Val'Ur was sat at the Generals table inside the Hamurfelions' main tent, the Generals, Rahool, Ji'Roh and Tara either sat or stood around opposite her, her warriors waiting outside.

Upon the sight of her Ji'Roh had bowed – as did her Generals – relief covering his face; she would give him a proper greeting later, but in the circumstances of the moment all she could offer was a pat on the shoulder and a 'I'm glad you are safe'.

"We are most pleased to see you" Zara spoke thankfully to Val'Ur "I see the King's messenger found you well."

"Yes, as mine has found you" she smiled "So I assume this means we can make peace between our peoples at last, here and now."-she presented the message Tara had brought her-"As you can see from this, me and your King are very much aligned, and the butchers of Vilwood are being hunted down as we speak."

The tent went silent, and Val'Ur could sense something wasn't quite right, that there was something they knew which she didn't – perhaps what Rahool had hinted to.

"What is it?" she asked, a shred of fear in her mind.

"I'm afraid peace is more complicated now Lady – Chancellor – Ur" Zara replied sombrely.

"I'm confused" Val'Ur probed "I have shown you your King's words, his messenger and mine's testimony to our intent, Hamurfel exonerated from the Vilwood massacre; what would impede peace now?"-everyone hesitated to tell her-"Ji'Roh?"

"The Dred King is dead" Xürr replied bluntly before Ji'Roh could answer in a gentler fashion – Rahool shooting him an angry look for doing so "The bastard Nor'un murdered him, so says your messenger"-he gestured to Ji'Roh, who stood quietly to the side of Val'Ur-"He handed us the King's seal" he offered it to Val'Ur freely, and she took it in hand, studying it for herself a moment.

"Ji'Roh?" she asked of her friend "Are you sure the King fell?"

"I did not see it with my eyes for I had no choice but to flee for the tombs, but there was no indication, be it from the King or otherwise, that Nor'un would let him live after our attempt at escape; in any case, the King knew the risk, and when it came to it he chose to hold his ground to buy me time to escape, knowing he would most likely fall"-he paused as he looked for some comfort in the truth-"He seemed to have made peace with that, if that helps m'lady."

Val'Ur gave a nod of understanding, still looking upon the signet ring's seal, pain going through her heart, wanting to scream at the loss, wanting to wrap her arms around her friend, to hold him tight and thank him for his efforts, but found herself unable to do either.

"Thank you Ji"-it was all she could manage-"Roselia will be most proud of you – before you ask, she is fine and doing well, and growing large with your child."

He gave a thankful smile and bowed, before letting more pressing matters and conversation continue.

"What of Amira? Is my beloved safe?" Val'Ur enquired eagerly, her brow furrowed in thought and worry.

"There is no indication he'd hurt or allow harm come to her; all love the True Queen, and even if he didn't, all of Hamurfel would fall upon him if he but laid the lightest of touch upon her" Zara reassured her.

"Seems Nor'un's keeping those Blackwood doctors caring for her, though one assumes they are on a short leash now" Xürr added.

"So what is our next move?" Rahool asked, eager to put his fist through Nor'un "The longer we wait, the more entrenched his control over Akiro will be."

"As true as that is Rahool, we cannot just raid our own home" Zara cautioned, weary of her old comrade's disregard for fineness "There's the people, innocent Hamurfelions he may use as human shields or hostages – a situation we very much would like to avoid."

Val'Ur turned to Ji'Roh.

"Is there anything you can tell us about their positions, anything at all?"

"I'm sorry m'lady, as I've said to the Generals, I was only there a short time. All I can say is that before I made it to the King's Palace, the city guards seemed to be dispersed in groups of two, sometimes three, throughout the city, and their presence seemed largest in the markets – nothing that seemed out of the ordinary in that regard."

"That's something I suppose" Xürr muttered, crossing his arms "But Nor'un will be planning for us, seeing as he didn't stop you Ji'Roh."

"Would he expect the Orcs to march alongside us?" Rahool pondered "Because if not...that could turn things heavily in our favour."

"He might, he might not – did he learn the content of your message, that it asked for peace?" Zara asked Ji'Roh.

"No, the Blackwood physician – Samara – managed a distraction before he could."

"Then there's no reason for him to expect us" Mozin'Ra spoke with confidence "With our combined numbers and the slightest element of surprise, we could retake Akiro in less than a day."

"There's that famous Orcish confidence" Xürr almost laughed "But it's best not to underestimate Nor'un – better to be over prepared than under."

"Agreed" Val'Ur nodded "But with my warriors – both those accompanying me from Ebo and those already battle-hardened – fighting alongside you and your troops he could not possibly have the numbers to put up a long fight."

"Numbers are not everything Chancellor" Sira'Or counselled "Even if we stormed through their defensive lines, Nor'un would surely retreat into the King's Palace."

"Queen's Palace now" Xürr corrected "and that's if he doesn't stay in there from the start."

"With respect" Tara interjected, having been silently listening this whole time "Akiro, whilst the most defensible and fortified place in all of Hamurfel, can only be as unbreakable as those who defend it."

"What's your point, messenger?" Mozin'Ra asked.

"My point, General, is that whilst Nor'un has enough men to hold Akiro they are few in number – he has only enough to keep the citizens in line and barely anymore."

"She's right, which is why he was trying to cause mass casualties upon our ranks" Zara added "And why he betrayed us to the Orcs"-Mozin'Ra shifted uneasily in his chair-"No offence."

“We will talk of that dishonour later” Val’Ur promised “But if I understand you, this means a single frontal assault would suffice?”

“I’d suggest we move in from the south”-Zara drew the plans with her hands on the table as she spoke-“and have a detachment secure the Eastern Pass – Nor’un’s only means of escape or reinforcement, if there is any for him – then we pincer in on the Palace.”

“What of the Palace itself?” Sira’Or asked.

“That we’ll have to be a bit inventive on” Val’Ur answered “It is built to outlast any siege.”

“We shall continue this talk later” Zara stood up “but, with your word Chancellor Ur, we should inform our men of our new directive.”

“Yes” Val’Ur nodded, rising from her seat also “Mozin’Ra, have my tent made up for the night and order the others to prepare for the journey north.”-she paused-“And have a group of warriors guide our injured home – you should go with them Ji’Roh, you have done enough.”

“Thank you m’lady; I’ll be sure to carry your message of unity back to Ebo.”

*

Val’Ur left the tent she had granted Sierra and Tara, having taken the time to talk with them, to meet with the Generals to further discuss their battle plans.

There was a moment of silence – bar the sound of countless troops and warriors preparing for the march north – Sierra resting her elbows upon the wooden table, hands clasped tightly together as she waited for Tara to say something, until she felt compelled to ask.

"Tara?" she began, Tara looking beyond the tent's walls – presumably towards home, to Akiro and the stolen throne "How're you holding up?"

Tara turned her head to face her, her gaze following slowly, but she did not reply.

"The loss of your King...from how you've spoken on him, I can tell it must hurt."

Tara took in a deep, audible breath, releasing it slowly before then replying.

"When last I saw him, he had given me my orders, my mission, set me on a journey that led me to you. It – I – carried his hope for peace, that he might reason with kinder hearts"-she leaned over her own hands, looking down at them like they might tell her the answer to her troubles-"He was angry, rage filled at times. Sometimes to the point where...no, that doesn't matter; he loved his people, and he commanded loyalty. He had my loyalty; he still does. I just, to lose him – let alone to Nor'un! Nor'un who was seen as a friend to him, Nor'un, 'Sword of Akiro'...I...I feel sick."

"Given what our now ex-Chancellor has done, I can understand the sense of betrayal" Sierra sympathised, unsure of how to comfort her.

"But he was the Dred King, brother to the True Queen! Flawed as he may have been, he ruled from a place of love!"-she hammered down on the table with a clenched fist-"His end...he did not deserve to end that way. It's so unjust..." Tara cried; the

King had shown her kindness when she had lost her dear Elisa, even though she wasn't noble or of high standing.

Sierra put her hands around Tara's still clenched fist, Tara looking up at her as she did, her wet, teary eyes mirrored in the empathic blue and green of her unlikely love.

"They'll get him Tara; Nor'un won't get away with what he has done."

"But, what good is that to the Dred King now? He's gone...he's gone..."

"Then...think of the True Queen, of Val'Ur – even yourself – you will all get to see him face justice"-Sierra moved to her knees before Tara, taking both her hands in hers now-"I cannot take the pain of loss from you my love, I wish I could but I can't. I can listen, I can offer words to soften your soul. I can – and will – march with you into Akiro. Just know that I am here, that I love you, and that I will always be there to lean on when you need me."

Tara's cheeks ran wet with tears; so did Sierra's.

"...hold me" Tara croaked through her tears.

Sierra did, and there they stayed embraced, until there were no more tears to give.

CHAPTER THIRTY-EIGHT

Siege of Akiro, Hamurfel

The Hamurfelion and Orcish forces moved as one great wave upon the sands of Akiro, even if there was still some unease amongst their ranks at marching side-by-side with those who had been their enemies for so long. Zara's forces flanked either side of what had been the Orcish central force, Xürr's heavy horse leading the vanguard alongside Val'Ur and her following of Kaymar's warriors; Rahool rode alongside General Sira'Or, trading tales of battle and combat.

Sierra and Tara moved alongside General Mozin'Ra, Tara aiding him with knowledge of the topography that surrounded the Palace; Sierra close by her side, driven mainly by a desire to keep her safe.

"How're your nerves?" Sierra asked Tara as the city came into view.

"Honestly? Better – calmer – than I expected; much calmer than when I told you who I really was in fact"-Tara looked at her warmly-"I thought...I was so worried you'd abandon me, break my heart..." Tara trailed off as she saw the city's warning beacons alight, knowing what it would mean.

Sierra noticed them too; they all did, in quick succession, and as the whole mass of troops and warriors picked up speed in response, Sierra asked one last thing of Tara."

"Tara, stick by my side, no matter what."

"Always Sierra, but in war all I can do is try."

*

Nor'un cursed at the sight of the beacon's fire.

"How many?" he asked the outer-guardsman who had been sent from the city's walls.

"All of them" the man replied apologetically through his panting.

"What do you mean *all*?"

"Both General Zara and General Xürr's forces march alongside Orcish warriors, they-"

Nor'un raised his hand, signalling for him to be quiet as he closed his eyes in thought.

“Gather my Commanders”-he turned to another of his men-“seal the walls, and let loose every arrow in our arsenal.”

He knew they would have to fall back to the Palace, that the city would be breached – with the Orcs on Zara’s side their numbers alone would be too much to contain. He pondered whether it would come down to him and the True Queen; ultimately, he decided he would be true to his word, even if breaking it would save him.

Kalib stayed hidden in the shadow of a clay pillar, listening to the situation at hand. After waiting for Nor’un and his men to leave to deal with the returning forces and their newfound Orcish allies, he snuck back to Samara in their secured quarters – now guardless in the panic.

“Well?” she asked him as he closed the door behind him.

“Things are about to get real messy” he exhaled, wiping his brow with a cuffed sleeve “The King’s forces have returned, and the Orcs are marching alongside them.”

“Oh” Samara replied, furrowing her brow in thought “Well, now we know the messenger made it, that the King did not die in vain.”

“Perhaps we should barricade ourselves in with the True Queen” Kalib suggested “Stop Nor’un from using her as a bargaining piece?”

“Yes” Samara nodded, rising to her feet “But first, let us aid the Hamurfelions in retaking their home.”

“How?”

“By ensuring there’s an easy way into the Palace”-she moved past him, carrying a table knife and opening up the door-“Bring our supplies Kalib; I'll meet you in the True Queen's chamber when I can."

*

There was blood everywhere.

Unholy torrents of arrows had rained down for much of the last hundred yards to the city walls, and many Orcish and Hamurfelion heavy horse lay felled as the gateway to the city buckled beneath the weight of two armies. The Orcs of the central bulk had climbed the walls, throwing Nor'un's archers from them as Val'Ur and Xürr led the main forces through a now wrecked defensive gateway.

Sierra staggered back to her feet, her warhorse fleeing into the distance, arrows still embedded in its side – she would need to find him later. She looked for Tara, but all she could see was the blood and the dead; she had lost sight of her as they had all tried to protect themselves from the arrows. She had tried to protect Tara, but as her horse was struck in the onslaught it bucked in pain, throwing her to the ground, everything becoming blurry as her head impacted the ground.

"Sierra?" Mozin'Ra called, a small detachment with him "Send word to Val'Ur that we move to secure the Eastern Pass!" he gestured towards the city and where she would find Val'Ur.

Sierra nodded, picking up her sword, looking around once more for Tara before running into the city.

*

Nor'un watched from a window on the upper floor of the Palace, his Commanders following his plan to the letter. He had had them station small batteries of troops nestled amongst the civilians' homes – archers mostly upon the upper floors – to divide his enemies and pick them off one-by-one; the hope was to slow their advance and whittle down their numbers so that they might be weakened enough for a counter attack.

It was a dishonourable way to fight, and endangered the civilians, those whose homes had be 'requisitioned' even more so; Nor'un wasn't about to let that stop him, not now, not when he was so close to his goal.

He turned back to the last of his Commanders still inside the Palace.

"Are the barricades ready?" he asked.

"Yes King Nor'un, and thirty-eight men stand ready at your direct command."

Nor'un smiled, confident in his strategy; he didn't earn his reputation and rank from losing, so why would now be any different?

"Sir, there is one thing" the Commander added "The Blackwood doctors have barricaded themselves in the True Queen's chambers."

Nor'un laughed.

"Leave them be; there'll be time enough to deal with them afterwards."

*

Sierra jogged through the streets, weaving past skirmishes, narrowly avoiding the odd arrow and an ambush that burst from a civilian's home as Zara hammered into them alongside some of Val'Ur's elite warriors.

"Mozin'Ra is securing the Eastern Pass!" Sierra informed them as the last of the ambushers were slain.

Zara gave a nod of acknowledgement, before continuing onward towards the Palace; Sierra returning to her jog through the city streets, struggling to navigate the twists and turns of the city as she looked for Val'Ur and Tara. She passed more skirmishes, and the aftermaths of successful and failed ambushes from Nor'un's men, until she found herself in one of the city's main markets, looking around, trying to think of which offshooting path to take when she heard a voice call out to her.

"Sierra!"

She turned on the spot, looking to the north-western street the voice had come from.

"Tara!" she called back, relief washing over her as she ran towards her.

Tara ran too, before stopping abruptly, skidding through the dirt as she saw an arrow fly out from a second-floor window, shouting for Sierra to duck.

She could hear the thud of its impact from where she stood.

Sierra yelled in pain, losing her footing as she was toppled by the impact, looking down at the wooden shaft that had ruptured through just below her shoulder as she pushed herself up to a crawl and tried to scramble behind the closest merchant's stall for cover. Tara ducked, leapt and dove from where she had stood, to and from cover as arrows barely missed her, until she found herself sat next to Tara.

"Tara..." she leaned over her, looking over the arrow's entry and exit points.

"It's okay, it's okay" Sierra laughed in pain, trying to calm Tara, instinctively caressing the side of her beloved's face "I think it missed the bone."

"I need to get you out of here" Tara looked at her love with fear.

"What of Akiro? Hamurfel?"

"None of it matters, none of it is worth a damn if you're not here with me!"

Sierra placed a hand upon Tara's waist, pulling her close for a quick, gentle kiss.

"Tara, I 'aint going nowhere"-she began to get to her feet, or as much as she could whilst staying behind cover-"But we must see this through, and let Val'Ur know the Eastern Pass is being secured."

"The archer" Tara reminded her.

"Ah yes"-Sierra readied her sword in her good arm-"Mind distracting him whilst I get a little closer, my love?

*

Val'Ur pushed the man off the end of Soulbreaker, taking the shortest of moments to stare up at the palace she was now so close to.

"Chancellor Ur!" a female voice called to her "The Eastern Pass is being secured by Mozin'Ra as we speak!"

"Good" she nodded, seeing Tara and Sierra, whose chainmail was stained with blood – some from her shoulder wound, some clearly not her own "You two can retreat with the wounded; send Zara and Xürr my way if you see them!"

"Retreat?" Sierra questioned "But the fight still rages!"

"Stay if you must; I offer you this chance to leave the fight out of respect for your love – I will not let Nor'un do to you what he may – or has – done to me."

The two looked at each other as Val'Ur turned to one of her warriors.

"Well?" Sierra asked Tara, her mismatched eyes searching her expression.

"I did give my word to my King" Tara replied, unsure and looking to Sierra for guidance.

"Then for Hamurfel" Sierra gave a reassuring smile "And for the glory of the Orc Isles!"

"No" Tara leaned her head against Sierra's "For us, For the Dred King, For the True Queen Amira."

"Aye" Sierra yelled with her as they began their search for the Hamurfelion Generals "For love!"

*

Samara crept out from the low window that had aided the King and Ji'Roh's escape, her right hand holding a now blood-stained knife, looking for those that would fight – and were fighting – against Nor'un, the sounds of clashing metal and war cries echoing from every direction she turned. It took her only a few minutes to find a cabal of Orcs and Hamurfelions who stood on the same side.

"Wait!" she called to them as they moved to aid Val'Ur's attempt to breach the Palace's main doors.

"Declare yourself!" Xürr demanded, his and Zara's group holding position.

"I am Samara Prime, current physician to the True Queen" she identified herself "I was hired by the Dred King himself before Nor'un-"

"How is our Queen?" Zara interrupted, desperate for news.

"She is safe – my partner Kalib has barricaded himself in her room with a handful of her loyal servants, but there will be time to talk later"-she gestured to whence she came-"Nor'un has secured the doors, and has men waiting to ambush and fire upon all who try to enter; I have a way in."

Xürr and Zara looked at each other, just as Sierra and Tara came running up to them.

"Generals, Val'Ur needs you" Sierra panted, one hand grasping at her aching wound.

"They're about to attempt to breach the Palace doors" Tara continued, finishing Sierra's sentence.

"Samara" Zara turned to her "How quickly can you get us inside?"

"Minutes at most" she replied "But we must go now, whilst there is still the opportunity."

"Tara, see that Val'Ur waits for one of us or our men to give her a signal to launch her attack – Nor'un has his men waiting to ambush her"-Tara nodded, before her and Sierra began racing back to Val'Ur-"Xürr – everyone – follow Samara."

*

Nor'un knew something was wrong by the sound of fighting coming from within the Palace walls, even before one of his men came running into the war-room, steadying himself upon the doorframe.

"Sir, Orcs have breached the walls of the Palace from some unseen place, and the Generals are with them!"

"Zara and Xürr?"

The man nodded.

Nor'un cursed.

"Put all of our forces on securing the main doors – DO NOT allow them the opportunity for reinforcements."

*

Zara and Xürr marched through the hallways of the Palace, the Orcish warriors, and a few of Xürr's troops who had joined them, had now splintered off to open the main doors and deal with the would-be ambushers and the archers on the upper floors. The two Generals were headed for the Throne Room, reasoning – as they knew him well – that would be where Nor'un would choose to make his last stand.

"I take it we're not taking him prisoner?" Xürr asked as the eastern door to the Throne Room drew close.

"No" Zara almost hissed "He did not spare our King, I – we – will not spare him."

As they kicked open the door, rushing in, they were met with the sight of Nor'un sat upon his stolen throne.

"Zara. Xürr." He greeted them, rising from his seat with no real haste, the sword that had been resting upon his lap now firm in his hand.

"Traitor!" Zara spat in reply as she marched towards him.

"Never did like you Nor'un" Xürr mocked as he moved to Nor'un's flank and cut off any means of escape "So I'm going to enjoy this just that much more."

"Enough words, Generals"-Nor'un readied his stance-"Show me how worthy you are of your titles."

*

Val'Ur stood behind one of the red sandstone pillars as arrows continued to fall upon them, waiting for a signal from Zara or her men.

"You sure they made it inside?" she shouted to Tara, who was behind another pillar – with Sierra – on the other side of the path that led to the main doors.

"As sure as I can be" she replied, glancing around the pillar quickly, an arrow thundering into the ground bedside her as she pulled herself back behind cover.

Just then, several wailing screams could be heard, followed by an equal number of heavy, meaty thuds of something hitting the ground from a great height.

Val'Ur tentatively looked around the edge her pillar, seeing Nor'un's archers dashed upon the stone steps of the Palace, and an Orc warrior waving to them with a makeshift flag made of his tabard from a window above; this was the sign they'd been waiting for.

With that Val'Ur roared, rallying her people and allies to storm the Palace, Soulbreaker raised high.

Even centuries after, people would speak of the overwhelming strength that emanated from her in that moment.

*

Nor'un kicked back Xürr, striking Zara across the temple with the hilt of his sword, knocking her to the floor. Xürr, still winded, tried desperately to return a swing at him before Nor'un could return to a sure-footing, but alas he was not quick enough. They parried each other's blows, strike after strike echoing through the throne room like thunder, until at last Nor'un finally managed to disarm Xürr, throwing him atop Zara as she struggled to get back to her feet, blood oozing over her left eye. Nor'un readied to finish them both off once and for all, when a powerful voice called out.

"Nor'un!" Val'Ur roared as she entered the throne room, her speed as she approached him matched only by her poised determination "What have you done with my beloved?"

Nor'un glanced from Val'Ur to the two Generals and back again, weighing if he would have enough time to dispatch them before she could fall upon him with her unusual Orcish blade.

"Val'Ur, the True Queen is safe and unharmed I assure you"- he decided it was best to try and turn her to his cause-"And when she is well and strong enough I will gladly return the rule of Hamurfel to her."

"Is that what you promised the King before murdering him?" she seethed calmly as she drew close, her trusty Soulbreaker in hand.

Nor'un's brow furrowed in a cold frown.

"Do not make the mistake of crossing me Lady Ur; none of us want our people at war."

"Says the man that helped start it"-her voice was firm-"and it is no mistake"-she smiled menacingly, ignoring his threat as she thrust a quick and vicious strike at him; although he managed to deflect the blow it cost him his sword, which was shattered into a rain of shards by Soulbreaker's might, leaving him with less than half a crooked edge to defend himself with-"It is an act of justice!"

Nor'un back-stepped as swiftly as he could without looking, retreating to where he could as she advanced upon him; there was no mistaking the look in her eyes, and he knew one of them would fall this day.

She swung at him in a large arc, he dodged to the side before swinging his shattered blade back at her, catching her lightly upon her wrist armour as she deftly spun out of his reach, putting all her weight and force upon her back foot and leapt at him, all her might going into a sideways thrust that cut him across his chest, dragging his chainmail into and through him.

Nor'un staggered back a few steps in reflex from such an impact, before then dropping to his knees; his shattered half-sword clattering to the ground as he did.

Val'Ur walked over to him, his breathing heavy and laboured as he held himself up by his fists. She waited a moment, watching him, the only sound his exhausted, degrading breath as Zara and Xürr staggered to their feet, Xürr steadying Zara with her arm around his shoulder.

"It is done?" Zara gasped, unable to see out of her left eye.

"Not yet" Val'Ur replied, still looking down at Nor'un "Why? Why do all this?" she asked him.

He managed to look up at her, his body defeated even if his mind was not.

"For Hamurfel. For the people" he wheezed "The Dred King was but a fool...knew only anger...led to war..."

Val knelt before him, Soulbreaker still in hand.

"You see how this bloodshed was needless? You could have given him counsel."

"Was my...friend once...knew...he would not...listen."

"Amira would have. You know it. You just chose the path that satisfied your bloodlust, your hunger for power."-he stared at her, silent at the accusation-"You are no better than my father" she remarked as she got back to her feet "Generals, I leave this one to your judgment; I fear I would go down a dark path if it were left up to me."

"Understood" Xürr nodded "But first, we should show his loyalists he is defeated; that should put an end to the remaining fight."

"Agreed" Val'Ur replied, dragging Nor'un towards the Palace entrance, thinking hard on not killing him for what he had done to his people, to Hamurfel, and most of all what he had done to her beloved's brother.

CHAPTER THIRTY-NINE

Queen's Chambers, Palace of the True Queen, Akiro

The sight of Nor'un crippled and dying had drained his supporters of any remaining will they had left to fight, choosing instead to surrendered; and whilst they would be tried for their treachery, Xürr and Zara would not sentence them to death, on the behest of True Queen Amira. Instead they would be put to work in the mines for the betterment of all of

Hamurfel, so that they might redeem themselves in time; a gift they were most thankful for.

At this moment Zara stood at the back of Amira's chamber, next to Xürr, Sierra and Tara, her left eye covered with an eyepatch and still unsure if sight would return to it. Before them was Val'Ur, knelt by Amira's side as she sat up in her bed, still too weak to stand.

"...and your father, what of he?" Amira asked, audibly disheartened by all that had happened without her knowledge.

"He will be tried for treason, war crimes and the slaughter of Vilwood, alongside his conspirators" she replied, softly holding Amira's weak and shaking left hand.

"The 'corrupt Lords' and their lackeys?"

"Yes. All of them."

"And then? Imprisonment, something more severe?" Amira's eyes were concerned and soft, if a little tired.

"They...the people feel beyond betrayed-"

"As do mine, I'm sure" Amira gave a weary smile "We must do what we need to bring them peace...even if it hurts."

"It shouldn't hurt, he...he has done such evil things"-Val'Ur looked into the distance beyond her sight-"Why do I still care Amira?"

"Because you are not like him, or any of them; you are still good, kind...empathetic."-she looked up at Sierra and Tara-"These two brought you my brother's message?"

"Yes"-Val gestured for them to come over-"They were instrumental to liberating us all from this accursed war."

"You're too kind Chancellor Ur" Sierra said politely "We were but a messenger and her escort."

“With a message that if undelivered would have doomed all of Hamurfel” Amira responded, looking upon the pair with a nostalgia of sorts, seeing much of herself and Val in them “I understand you two are to wed?”

“Yes my Queen, that we are” Tara replied, a tad nervous “We...the events of this last year or so have taught me that we cannot wait for the things we love.”

“To think you found each other, on opposite sides of a war no less...”-she gave a glance to Val'Ur, lightly squeezing her hand with a smile-“I must give you a gift...a wedding present of sorts.”

“We're honoured Queen Amira” Sierra smiled “But we have each other, and that is enough.”

Amira gave a weak laugh.

“You are right; they do remind me of us, when we were younger” she sighed, Val'Ur smiling back at her as soft tears hung round the base of her eyes, before looking back at the two of them “But I must gift you something, it is only right...”-she beckoned Xürr over-“General Xürr, have it noted and ascribed that from this day forth that the messenger known as Tara is now of a noble line”-Sierra and Tara looked at each other in shock, unable to speak-“and shall forevermore hold the title Speaker in the Court of Hamurfel; you are now Lady Tara, Speaker of Hamurfel.”

Before Tara could even muster a response, Val'Ur added another gift.

“And you, Sierra of the Homeguard, from this day forth shall hold the title of Lady Sierra, the Obsidian Heart, Listener of the Orc Isles.”

Sierra clasped her hand around Tara's, the two of them rendered dumbstruck by this most unexpected of news, looking at each other a moment with the heartiest of smiles.

"I...we...we have no words" Tara managed to say at last.

"We need not your words, for your faces tell us all that needs be said" Val'Ur smiled as she got to her feet "Now, tell us; what arrangements were you thinking for your wedding?"

"Well, there was this one idea" Sierra grinned, looking at Tara, knowing in her heart that from this point on, there would be only light in their life together.

"Lady – Chancellor – Ur, my Queen" Xürr interrupted politely "I apologise, but before we focus on weddings, there is still the issue of the disputed lands."

"Yes, my father had planned on profiting heavily from the mines there once his other schemes had run their course; keeping all the gains to himself"-she almost spat at the thought of him, before turning to Amira-"Well my love, what do you think?"

All waited upon the word of the True Queen, whose honesty and kind heart still beat with strength in her frail state.

"No more war" she answered softly, her hand resting in Val'Ur's "No more senseless bloodshed."-she looked into Val'Ur's eyes-"Beloved, even if we were to marry – when we marry – our two peoples will want to remain their own."

"I'm sure the remaining Lords would agree with on that."

"So...I propose a compromise; the land shall remain forever *both* of ours – a union of Orcish industriousness and Hamurfelion custom."

"My love, how would that work?"

Amira gave a weak grin, a cheeky smile of one who sees as others do not.

"Either people may settle the land – but not unfairly so – and the mines will be jointly owned by the Court of Hamurfel and Chancellery of the Orc Isles, where the revenue shall be used for the protection of the people of Cairngor and its surrounding lands and, where possible, to foster trade and friendship between both peoples.

Val'Ur smiled, wanting desperately to kiss her, but held back until they could have a private moment.

"Trust you to think on a way of using a dispute to forge an alliance that will reinforce itself in perpetuity."

"A friendship" Amira corrected with a smile.

"I shall have the stewards write up a treaty" Xürr nodded in respect "Would you like to review it as it is written Chancellor Ur?"

"Have General Mozin'Ra oversee it; I'll read it with Amira once it is done."

With that he gave a small bow and left the room, giving Tara a nod of respect as he did.

"Zara" Amira called, the General coming over to her and kneeling by her bedside.

"Yes my Queen?"

Amira placed a hand upon Zara's shoulder.

"I am given to understand that Aka Nor'un did not give my dear, beloved brother a true burial. I fear I am..."-she gave a heavy breath-"I lack the strength to see to making it right myself; will you do him one last service, and see him laid to rest where he belongs?"

“I...It would be my honour” Zara replied, keeping herself from tearing up.

“I believe my father had rooms built for us in his tomb?”

“Indeed he did my Queen” Zara replied, near overcome with emotion due to her closeness to the Dred King and his father before him, feeling her voice crack a little – even if only she notice it “I will see to every detail personally.”

Amira gave her a sincere, thankful smile.

“You have been loyal to us for so long Zara – father always spoke highly of you; I would like to reward it.”

“There is no request I could make, and no reward needed, I assure you”-Zara had never felt so honoured, save for her wedding day-“I live to serve all of Hamurfel.”

Amira gave a weak, caring laugh.

“And serve it you have, and served it well, but...I cannot let your loyalty – your friendship and guidance – go unnoticed”-Amira’s face went sombre-“So, General Zara, defender of Akiro and the Dred throne, Protector of Hamurfel, I formally request that you become Regent Commander, extension of my will.”

Zara had no words.

“It is as much as I could ask any to do, but I know you Zara, this is as much a reward to you as it is responsibility.”

“But...I don’t know what to say” Zara felt flustered “I would gladly accept, but, would you not want your wife-to-be to lead Hamurfel in periods of your ill health?”

Amira looked to Val’Ur, and she to Amira.

“General Zara, I will always protect Hamurfel and its people, but the Orc Isles needs me to lead it out of where my father has dragged it”-she took her eyes off Amira a moment to look at Zara-“And when Amira is unwell I…Amira trusts you with her life Zara, and so so do I. If you need counsel I will give it gladly and swiftly, but Hamurfel needs someone to keep her steady and strong at all times.”

“If you both have confidence in me…then I accept this high responsibility gladly.”

“Then it is settled” Amira clapped lightly “We will have a ceremony a week from now – once we've dealt with Nor'un and his conspirators.”

“Speaking of ceremonies” Val'Ur grinned “We need to organise our wedding, and theirs”-she gestured back to Tara and Sierra-“Speaking of which, what request did you have of me?”

“Well” Sierra replied, still amazed by the current turn of things “I've heard of a place that is meant to bring good luck to those who wed there; a place of the setting sun?”

Val'Ur's smile widened.

“I know the place; leave it with me.”

CHAPTER FOURTY

1454, 2ND ERA
Sunset Cliffs, Ebo, Capital City of the Orc Isles
Eight months after War's End

The carved obsidian that made up the Sunset Cliffs was lighter and less imposing than that which made up the rest of the city, acting more as a backdrop, a canvas, upon which a sea of green and white was painted, with odd droplets of light violet colours scattered elegantly about it. It was a secluded place, high up and quiet, with a view that stretched for leagues towards the coast, and sheltered from any strong breeze; a perfect place to marry, with a few choice guests.

Tara softly stroked the stem of one of the violet flowers as she lifted its head to smell its fragrance; it was a shade darker than the rest, and she could swear its sweet scent was more pungent too, if not by much. As she returned her gaze to her surroundings she reflected upon the white silks from Hamurfel – which were so fine you could almost see through them – and how they seemed to compliment the Orcish green cotton almost as if they had been fated to be together; a good sign, so she thought.

"Nervous?" Val'Ur asked as she came up beside her, dressed in her formal buttoned jacket with the gold-trimmed shoulder patches.

"Should I be?" Tara smiled "I'm glad you made it; wasn't sure you would."

"I could not miss the marriage of those who helped reunite me with my Amira before...Well, even if we are not as close as friends, we share a bond; and I am honoured you would ask me to bear witness" Val'Ur replied, almost stumbling at the thought of her dear departed love, gently checking she had not smudged her face-paint.

Tara gave a smile and a nod to that, looking back out over the wall that lined the cliff, watching the Sun arc lower in the sky.

"Won't be long until sunset" she sighed "Sierra is waiting next to the priests, isn't she?"

"So you are nervous" Val'Ur laughed "Yes, and I dare say she is nervous too; I left Rose and Ji'Roh with her, figured it best to leave her someone other than the priests to talk to."

"Aye" Tara looked down at her dress, a traditional Hamurfelion wedding garb of folded silk that spiralled around and down her figure which fanned out into a teardrop shaped skirt that hovered just above the floor, the tops of her arms and shoulders covered in a fine transparent weave. She wore her brown-red hair down, her curls lying intimately across either side of her shoulders, and in place of her usual headscarf was a transparent flow of frilled fine fabric that covered the top and upper back of her hair. In most other settings she would feel uneasy being dressed in something like this, her hair so free before so many people, but today? Today she felt beautiful, strong.

"Right" she said, taking a deep breath, her locket cool against her chest "I guess it's time."

Sierra stood nervously before the two priests – one Hamurfelion, the other a traditionalist Orc – as Roselia tried her best to distract and calm her; usually with comical tales of her baby boy, and usually at Ji'Roh's expense. She absently tapped her hand against her side as she waited, her nerves starting to get the better of her. She thought on how beautiful a place this was, especially as the Sun lowered itself toward the horizon, and pondered whether it would do Tara justice; she hoped so. Her dress was a Warrior's formalwear; it was a deep, almost vibrant red with a hoodless cloak fastened to her by a cloth pauldron, her long shirt and trousers fastened together with a fine leather belt. Her parents sat at the front of the small mass of friends and acquaintances – and General Xürr, who came on behalf of the Hamurfelion Court – her mother giving her a reassuring smile, her eyes betraying her excitement at her daughter's wedding; her father was rather more stoic, as was his way, but she could see it in his eyes, and in that slightest of smiles that would go unnoticed by most, that his heart was filled with joy. They had taken the news far better than she had expected when she told them those months ago, though they had voiced their displeasure at having not been at least introduced to Tara beforehand; ultimately they congratulated them, and were pleased with Tara becoming their daughter's wife.

Sierra was musing on her and Tara's future when the wedding announcer pulled the strings on her lute, signalling the coming of the bride, and felt her heart skip a beat. The priests stood ready next to one another, each holding an ancient text from their respective Temples, each of which were bookmarked so they knew where one would take over from the other, and Roselia took her place next to Ji'Roh a few rows in from the front. Sierra looked down the aisles of seats and people, watching as Tara's silhouette came up upon the silk curtains at the back, and then, as they were pulled open for her to walk through, Tara walking towards her.

She had not seen her in her wedding dress until this moment, and as such felt herself weak at the knees upon seeing

Tara in such elegance, feeling tears of joy she could barely keep back from smearing her ceremonial face-paint as her heart fluttered excitedly. She could not help but marvel at her, almost disbelieving how beautiful she looked, and how effortlessly she glided up the aisle. Tara stopped before the priests, turning to face Sierra, who took her hands in hers, the pair of them looking deep into each other's eyes as the priests began reading from their scriptures. The two of them could read each other, silently talking with their eyes, and the subtle expressions of love and joy etched upon their faces; they were in love, and by Oblivion that love shined bright that day.

Finally, the priests finished their part, wrapping an off-pink ribbon around their arms – a symbol of the joining of their hearts and entwining of their lives – and all that remained of the ceremony was for the two brides to kiss. They leaned in close, each leaning their foreheads softly against each other, their noses just touching as they took a nervous moment to breathe, before finally Tara leaned in, embracing her love in a soft, emotional kiss that filled her with that excited butterfly-like feeling, their guests giving a supportive applause as Sierra's father held her mother as she cried the happiest of tears.

As the sun set, the last ebbs of light peering over the horizon, Tara and Sierra held one another; Tara finding great comfort in Sierra's hands around her waist.

"I love you, my beautiful Warrior" She sighed, looking at her love lovingly.

"And I you, my Hamurfelion messenger" Sierra replied as she leaned in close, gently embracing her with a soft kiss upon her lips "I shall forever be grateful that your King sent you to deliver his message; to think how we would never have met had the war never begun."

"Perhaps" Tara cooed softly as she turned to see the ending sunset "But it matters not; so long as you are always there to hold my hand, all things are well."

"My ladies" Val'Ur interrupted politely, as she and Xürr held a large lantern, the entwined symbols of Hamurfel and the Orc Isles etched upon its papery shade "General Xürr and I have a special gift for you both."

"A lantern?" Sierra asked, thankful but bemused.

"Yes" Xürr smiled "Etched with the symbols of our two peoples entwined as one, just as you two are."

"If you release it together it will bring you eternal luck" Val'Ur added "Or so say the priests."

"Either way it'll look pretty, especially as it overtakes the sunset" Tara smiled a thank-you, turning back to Sierra "Well, my love?"

With that the two of them held either side of the lantern as Val'Ur lit its flame, feeling it wanting to pull away as the orange heat hit its papery sides.

Sierra looked at Tara, and she back at her, the both of them making the very same wish as they gently lifted the lantern and let it go. All of them watched as the orange orb of light slowly made its way higher, projecting soft shadows of its etchings upon the cliffs, until finally it hit a pocket of wind and was blown towards the coast, replacing the sun as the only light in the sky, all the while Tara and Sierra held each other's hand, smiling at all that which was yet to come.

II

"There is another gift for you both" Val'Ur said, untying her sword from her belt; it took them both a moment to realise what she meant.

"Your sword?" Sierra asked in shock, looking her deep in the eyes.

"Her name is Soulbreaker" Val'Ur smiled, holding the blade flat across her palms "She was my mother's, and my grandfather's before her, and has kept me safe for so long; it is time she protected someone new."

"We can't possibly accept" Tara tried to decline politely; such a personal thing should stay with those who would cherish it more, so she thought.

"Truly, Chancellor Ur, it is a...it's a gift beyond measure" Sierra added.

Val'Ur smiled.

"See, there's yet more of the reason you two deserve it; love like yours – humble and enduring – reminds me of Amira and I – and such love is deserving of protection"-Sierra and Tara looked at each other with hesitance-"I have no one to entrust it to now, none who needs it – Please, accept it as a token of my respect."

Sierra tentatively took hold of Soulbreaker by its hilt, and having unsheathed it, raised it aloft, high above their heads; the light from the lantern and newly lit candles glinting across its shimmering edge.

She felt tears in her eyes, her other hand holding Tara's.

"For the honour of Blackwood" she whispered quietly, a *Shadow* going unseen in the dark.

*

Always, there is a beginning. Always, there is an end.
It *knew this.* It *knew more than most; more than any should.*
A lantern rises softly, and in its shadows It *stayed hidden.*
It *watched, turning its attention to the entwined loves below.*
Unobserved, mist-like tendrils of Shadow *tightened and wound in the* Dark *in place of a heart's flutter.*
It *saw the breaker of souls, sheathed in ceremonial covering.*
It*'s attention turned to countless leagues north, looking upon a mountain of immeasurable size, at an alcove barely formed.*

It *waited.*

South Havaskus
Akiro
Hamurfel
Northern Pass
Blackwood
Havai Forrest
Bahvil
Bahvain
Draymour
Cairngor
Vilwood
Falketh
Tyros
Yarmor
Borvain
Kromahr
Ebo
Orc Isles

ABOUT THE AUTHOR

H. Sulfwin grew up admiring the heathered hills and rolling mountains of Scotland, often going on long walks and hikes and getting lost (not literally, thankfully) in the green forests and woodland, and the great rocky boundaries between lochs, waterfalls and the peaks of mountains, admiring the castles and villages as they were passed. This, combined with a love of storytelling that started from a young age and a passion for medieval knights and dragons, led ol' Sulfwin down the path of becoming an author.

OTHER BOOKS BY H. SULFWIN

www.ingramcontent.com/pod-product-compliance
Lightning Source LLC
Chambersburg PA
CBHW030535310726
48979CB00010B/1919/J
* 9 7 8 1 8 3 9 2 4 0 0 4 1 *